I0571978

Table of Contents

Seaside Series Trilogy

Romance Novellas

Sandra W. Burch

*"For I know the plans I have for you," declares the LORD,
"plans to prosper you and not to harm you,
plans to give you hope and a future." ~ Jeremiah 29:11*

Seaside Haven

Book 1 in the Seaside Series

Chapter One

Thunder rolled overhead as rain spat like gunfire on Seaside's sandy beachfront. Mother Nature's fury, however, was no match for the emotions churning inside Sierra Ramstad. Unmindful of the storm, she continued to walk. In the pocket of the red raincoat she wore, she fisted her slender hand around the crumpled piece of paper and recalled its content.

Miss Ramstad:

I will be arriving home tomorrow for an extended stay. Please have my room ready.

Phoenix Chamberlain

Two curt sentences that had her blood boiling.

Phoenix Chamberlain, III, heir to the Chamberlain fortune, was coming home, as he'd put it, to recuperate after the car accident he'd been involved in three months earlier.

If the news reports she'd read about his accident was even remotely accurate, then Sierra supposed she should feel sorry for him. Along with a concussion and a dislocated shoulder, he'd broken his ankle and shattered the femur in his left leg. Three months out and the man was in the midst of a long and painful recovery. Even so she didn't want him mending here, and possibly meddling in the day-to-day operations of Seaside Haven Resort.

Phoenix's family had a large home outside of Atlanta, Georgia, as well as an assortment of plush real estate sprinkled around Europe. Why hadn't he picked one of those places to recuperate? Surely they would be more accommodating to Phoenix's entourage who enabled his larger-than-life existence.

Why choose Seaside Haven? This wasn't his home. It was *hers*! While Phoenix had spent the past few years jet setting around Europe, living off a sizable trust fund and enjoying the life of the rich and famous, Sierra had been working to turn an old and nearly forgotten inn into a resort that offered five-star accommodations, panoramic views, and above all, excellent service.

Now Phoenix was returning and he wanted his room readied. It was Sierra's understanding that he hadn't visited the resort since his childhood. So she'd made the owner's private room on the main floor her own, and turned the adjacent apartment into a luxury suite that commanded a substantial sum of money to occupy it.

Muttering words that were muffled by the wind, she stopped and looked back in the direction she had come. The cedar shingled resort stood four stories tall, given the pilings that raised it above sea level to protect it from flooding. Her gaze skimmed the balconies that stretched out from each room to maximize the view. Even though it was early afternoon, the lights burned brightly in the windows of guests waiting out the storm.

Home.

Phoenix might refer to it as such, but for Sierra it truly was her home. It was here she'd come after her nasty divorce. The warm sunshine and the sense of purpose had ushered her back from the brink of despair.

With a reluctant sigh, Sierra headed back. Other guests would be arriving soon and that meant she had a job to do. Right now, her priority was to see that all new arrivals were settled in their rooms. Once that task was completed, she'd figure out her own accommodations for the duration of Phoenix's stay.

By the time she reached the resort, any part of her body that wasn't covered by the raincoat was drenched. She had hoped to have enough time to change into dry clothes and do something with her hair before any guests arrived, but a pearl white Cadillac Escalade with dark tinted windows was pulling up at the main entrance as she came around the sand dune.

The driver hopped out, as did another man who came around from the passenger side. Both were big and robust. It wasn't a surprise to see bodyguards as a lot of the resort's guests were Hollywood A-listers or business moguls. Before either man could reach the handle, the rear driver side door swung open.

Sierra covered her mouth with the palm of her hand, but a gasp still escaped.

Phoenix Chamberlain, III.

She had never met him in person. They had exchanged emails a couple of times a month, and occasionally a phone call. But he'd never come for a visit. Now here he was. And he wasn't at all what Sierra had expected.

Every photograph she had seen of him on social media showed a handsome young man with wavy, black hair, deep set dark brown eyes, a carefree smile and a body toned to perfection under the capable tutelage of a well-paid professional trainer.

Meanwhile, the man trying to exit the SUV's rear seat was thin and fragile. The dark smudges under his eyes made it clear that he hadn't been getting much sleep despite many hours spent in bed. And his rigid posture and pinched features indicated he was far from carefree.

"I'll get the wheelchair, Mr. Chamberlain," said the man who'd come around from the front passenger side.

"No! I'll walk," he snapped in an angry rasp that carried over the howling wind.

"But, Mr. Chamberlain…" the driver began, only to be shouted down.

"I said I'll walk, Tommy! I'm not an invalid!"

Phoenix had to use his hands to manipulate his left leg over the threshold. He swung his right leg out the door without much effort. Then, lowering himself to the running board, he eased his feet to the ground. He held a cane in one hand and used the other to grip the door frame. Unfortunately, neither support was enough. A mere second after both of his feet were on the pavement, his left knee buckled. The man he'd called Tommy caught Phoenix under his arms before he hit the pavement. Loud cursing followed. The other man rushed forward, as did Sierra, determined to help.

"Who are you?" Phoenix barked, shaking off the hand that she had placed on his arm.

She pushed back the hood of the raincoat and offered what she hoped was a pleasant and professional smile. Despite the raincoat's hood, her golden blond hair was damp and her bangs were plastered against her forehead. As for makeup, she doubted what she'd applied that morning still lingered on her eyes and cheeks. Her feet were bare and spattered with wet sand. It was hardly the image she'd planned to portray when she first met him.

"I'm Sierra Ramstad."

Phoenix continued to stare at her as if she were something to be studied under a microscope.

"We've spoken on the phone and via email for several years now. I manage Seaside Haven."

"Of course you do." His gaze flickered down in seeming dismissal. Although he said it under his breath, she heard him when he added, "I had you pegged right."

So, he had preconceived notions of her, did he? That didn't come as a surprise. She had entertained plenty of her own where he was concerned. Still, it made her mad that, after a glance, he could marginalize her personally and probably professionally.

Sierra cleared her throat and drew herself up to her full height of five foot five. Since Phoenix was hunched over, it put them at eye level. When their eyes met she didn't as much as blink. Using her most professional tone, she told him, "I wasn't expecting you until tomorrow."

"I changed my mind."

"That's obvious!"

"I was in Atlanta visiting my mom…" His words trailed off and his expression hardened. "I'm here now. I trust that is not a problem, Miss Ramstad."

"No problem," she assured him with a stiff smile. "I just need to explain that your room isn't ready."

"Am I to wait out here until it is?" he questioned irritably.

Standing under the portico, they were protected from the worst of the storm, but the wind blew sideways splattering them with rain every now and again.

"Oh, of course not," she replied as heat crept into her face. She turned on her heel and walked toward the lobby entrance, calling over her left shoulder, "Right this way, gentlemen."

Phoenix allowed Tommy and Adam to assist him in the direction of the door. Another time, he would have felt bad about the way he'd talked to her. But unfortunately for her, both his usual good humor and his playboy charm were like his leg; fractured beyond repair. Or so the physicians said. But they were wrong. They had to be. He couldn't spend the rest of his life this way.

The doors opened announcing their arrival. The lobby looked different than he remembered from the last time Phoenix had been to Seaside Haven. Varying shades of blue and yellow dominated the color scheme, accentuated with white and a shade of tan that reminded Phoenix of sand. The glow of the table lamps gave the room a warm, welcoming ambiance despite the storm that raged outside.

He exhaled slowly and some of the tension left his neck and shoulders. He was a long way from relaxed but Phoenix knew he had made the right decision to come here.

He glanced around the room again. "This is really nice," he said to no one in particular.

"The remodeling was completed this spring. All of the rooms have been updated in a similar color scheme." Sierra cleared her throat. Her tone was almost defensive when she added, "I emailed you numerous photographs."

Truth be known, he probably hadn't opened the email attachments. He was too busy spending his trust fund to care, he thought with a mental grimace.

"Well, the photographs didn't do it justice," he exclaimed.

Nor, Phoenix admitted to himself, had the image he'd had of Sierra done her justice.

For the past few years, he'd signed her paychecks, skimmed over the monthly reports, and approved her capital investments all the while offering minimal input. He'd never laid eyes on the woman he'd entrusted his resort to. Until now.

Sierra had shed the raincoat and stood in front of the reception desk wearing a blue polo shirt adorned with the resort's logo and a pair of white shorts that stopped mid-thigh. Her legs were tanned and toned. Phoenix's gaze lifted to her small waist before rising to her breasts, which were just the right size to fill his hands.

He tore his gaze away from her, surprised he was gawking the woman as if he were a sex-crazed frat boy on spring break. At the same time, he was relieved by his reaction, as he'd felt dead for far too long.

"If you don't mind, I need to get off of my feet, Miss Ramstad." Pain turned his tone gruff.

"Yes, of course, Mr. Chamberlain." She gave a curt nod. "Please, follow me."

Pride demanded that he do so under his own power. No matter how slow that would make the going.

"Adam, help Tommy with my bags."

Adam Vinateri had been his personal trainer, now he worked as his physical therapist. But he didn't mind lending a hand when called on to do so. After all, he was paid well for little work since Phoenix regularly skipped his daily stretching and strengthening exercises.

Phoenix knew he needed to do the exercises. But knowing and doing them were two different things. Most days, he didn't bother to get out of bed, because physician after physician offered such a grim prognosis.

He shifted his weight from his good leg to his bad one. The pain was excruciating and he bit back a groan, wondering if it had been wise to swear off the narcotics the doctor prescribed. The pain pills made him feel brain dead and he was afraid that the state of oblivion might prove to be addictive.

His progress was slow and his gait uneven but at least he was walking on his own. Sierra turned around once, concern obvious in her expression, but she didn't offer any assistance. Apparently, his rude dismissal of her help had done the trick. And for that he was glad. Phoenix hated the way people treated him like an invalid.

Women had been among the worst offenders. That was one of the reasons he'd dissed the entourage of females that accompanied him at the chalet. As for his male friends, the number had dwindled substantially once it became obvious Phoenix no longer would be throwing any of the parties for which he had been known for.

Users, every last one of them. What did that say about him, Phoenix wondered? The only loyalty he commanded was among people such as Tommy and Adam and of course, Miss Ramstad, all of whom were on his payroll.

Behind the reception desk, a door led to a hallway. To the left were the business office and supply room. Phoenix remembered playing hide-and-seek in them when he visited his grandfather. The owner's bedroom was on the right. The door was closed and the word PRIVATE was engraved on a plaque affixed just below the peephole. After Sierra pulled a key from her pocket and opened it, Phoenix stepped over the threshold, expecting to be assailed with memories of his grandfather, the one person in his life whose love had been unconditional. But as in the lobby, nothing was as he remembered. Given his emotional state, he wasn't sure whether he was grateful for that or not.

The last time Phoenix had been inside of the room, the décor had been more masculine. It wasn't only the pale shade of paint on the wall, and the furnishings that made it seem feminine, it was the smell. The scent that lingered in the air was not that of his grandfather's Swisher Sweet cigars. Rather, it was a light and fresh scent. Her scent. He inhaled deeply, finding it comforting and arousing at the same time. He shoved the thought aside, only to have another take its place.

"Do you stay in here?"

Sierra frowned. "Yes, for the past few years. Room and board are one of the perks of the manager's job."

"I know that! But this room was my grandfather's. It is for the owner, Miss Ramstad."

Her tone was as incredulous as her expression. "But I told you…"

Phoenix cut her off. "I thought there was an adjacent room to accommodate the manager."

Sierra's mouth puckered at his statement, drawing Phoenix's attention to her plump lips that needed no added color to make them appealing.

"There is, or rather, there was. But since this room was empty all the time, I…that is, *we* decided it made more sense to turn the adjacent manager's room into a luxurious suite that could accommodate guests for an extended stay."

"*We* did?" Phoenix questioned.

Color rose in her cheeks. "I sent you several cost-benefit analysis reports and you said that you agreed with my suggestions."

"I remember now." Phoenix nodded, although he was damned if he could recall doing any such thing.

Every dime Sierra had invested in the resort had paid off, he decided. Whereas he had been reckless in the past, the risks she'd taken had been calculated and well planned. He might have approved her plans, but the ideas had been hers alone. Although Phoenix had a degree in Marketing and Management, one that he'd never had to use, he would be wise to learn from his very competent manager, Miss Ramstad.

"It's been full ever since," she chimed.

Which meant it was full now.

Phoenix appreciated her ability to turn unused space into a profitable one, but it did make for an awkward situation. He couldn't hold out any longer. "Where are you going to sleep, Miss Ramstad?"

Where was *she* going to sleep?

Sierra gritted her teeth and offered what she hoped passed for an unconcerned smile.

"I'll figure out something for the duration of your stay." As unspecified as that might be.

Phoenix staggered to the sofa and dropped heavily onto the plush cushions, his face drawn with a grimace. Sheer will power had kept him upright, of that she was certain. She might have admired his tenacity if it weren't accompanied by such a brusque disposition.

"Well, there must be at least one available guest room, right?" For the first time, he sounded more uncertain than he did ornery.

"No, we're full." She exhaled slowly. "Actually, we're booked for the rest of the season barring any last-minute cancellations." When Phoenix continued to gawk at her, she added, "It's been an excellent summer so far. Revenues are up by…"

He cut her off abruptly. "Well, you can't sleep in the lobby, Miss Ramstad!"

Sierra had made the same determination, but her options were limited. The only alternative was…

Her gaze cut to the adjacent room where she exercised when the weather prevented her from walking on the beach. It had a futon that made into what her twin sister, Sienna, claimed was a comfortable bed. Her sister was the only overnight guest Sierra had entertained. On a sigh, she recalled her upcoming visit. She'd have to let her know plans had changed. Yet another disruption in her well-organized schedule.

"I'll stay in the exercise room," she said at last.

"No!" His tone made the single syllable sound final.

Sierra felt her blood pressure rise. The man certainly knew how to push her buttons. She didn't like being told what to do. Since her divorce, no man had dared, nor would she have tolerated it. She had a voice and these days she used it with impunity.

"It will be a tight fit," she admitted. Not to mention that she would have to figure out where to shower and stow her clothes, but at least it offered her more privacy than the resort's common areas.

Phoenix leaned his head back on the sofa and closed his eyes. Dressed in all black, a color that mirrored his mood, she couldn't help but notice how out of place he looked amid the array of colorful throw pillows. The taut line of his mouth and the way his brow creased made it clear that he was in pain.

"When was the last time you took a pain pill?" she quizzed. She tried to keep her tone neutral, careful to keep any concern from seeping into it.

"I quit those a few weeks ago," he mumbled. Just when she started to think that his decision stemmed from some macho man bull, he added, "They make me feel brain dead. The last thing I need is to become addicted to pain killers."

His reasoning was sound, even though his pain was left unmanaged.

The two men who accompanied Phoenix strode into the room. The driver was tugging a pair of suitcases that were large enough to hold Sierra's entire wardrobe. The other man pushed the wheelchair. A smaller bag was nestled on its seat with a garment bag draped over top of it. Sierra's stomach knotted. Phoenix had brought a lot of baggage, in more ways than one.

"Where do you want your things, Mr. Chamberlain?" the driver asked.

Without opening his eyes, Phoenix motioned with one hand in the direction of the closet. "Put them in there, Tommy."

"And mine, boss?" asked the guy pushing the wheelchair.

Phoenix did open his eyes now as he straightened in his seat. "I guess you will be here on the sofa, Adam. Since Miss Ramstad will be in the adjacent room."

Chapter Two

Phoenix waved a hand. "Not to be rude, but if you could move your belongings out of my room and be on your way, I'd appreciate it very much. I need to lie down."

He didn't wait for her to respond. He turned his head on the pillow and closed his eyes.

Sierra had been dismissed like the hired help she was. And his dismissal made her blood boil once more. It took an effort, but she managed to swallow her pride. "Sure, Mr. Chamberlain, I'd be happy to oblige."

Although the rooms were neat, she would have to change the linens on the bed before Phoenix used it. She'd planned to do that chore in the morning, as well as gather up her clothes and toiletries in anticipation of his arrival. But showing up early and bringing other guests had left her feeling inadequate.

When the driver exited the room, Sierra stepped into the adjacent doorway. Glancing around the room, she tapped a finger to her lips. The treadmill would have to be moved to the corner of the room in order to open the futon bed, which would also need clean linens. Same for the bedroom's pullout sofa, where Phoenix had assigned his therapist, Adam, to bunk.

As if reading her mind, Adam said from behind her, "I'm sorry for all of the inconvenience our stay is causing you."

Sierra turned, taking in his sweet smile. She guessed him to be a few years younger than her, which would put him in his early twenties. Despite his age, his face was almost boyish.

"It's no problem," she lied.

He let go of one of the wheelchair handles and extended his hand. "I'm Adam Vinateri."

"I'm Sierra Ramstad. It's nice to meet you, Adam."

He nodded. "Would it be okay if I kept my things in this room?

Sierra nodded and pointed across the room to a dresser. "If you'd like, you can put some of your things in there. And there's plenty of room in the closet if you need to hang up your clothes."

"Thanks. But I'm t-shirt and shorts kind of guy."

She nearly smiled.

Adam's simple wardrobe explained his medium sized suitcase while his boss had brought a pair of large suitcases as well as a garment bag. The designer labeled clothing inside of the bags wasn't the issue. The amount of clothing stated he was planning a far more extended stay than she'd assumed.

"This is a nightmare," Sierra muttered, momentarily forgetting about Adam.

"It's okay." Not surprisingly, Adam misunderstood what she meant and gave her a reassuring smile. Then motioning over his shoulder, he added, "He's not so bad, once you get to know him."

"I'm sure." Her attempt at sounding convincing fell far from short.

"Mr. Chamberlain is in a lot of pain right now," he insisted.

She nodded. "Phoenix told me he's not taking the pain medication that the doctors prescribed."

Adam leaned in closer and dropped his voice to barely above a whisper. "The accident has taken an emotional toll as well, although I doubt he'd admit it."

Sierra supposed she shouldn't find that surprising. Even the strongest people could succumb to depression.

"How bad is his injury?"

"Well, to be honest Ms. Ramstad, it's one of the worst I've seen. Major ligament damage in addition to the bone fractures. The doctors advised amputating it above the knee." Adam shook his head as he exhaled.

"Oh, my God!" Sierra gasped. "I had no idea it was so severe."

"Yes, he managed to keep that from being leaked to the press. His *friends...*" Adam snorted, as if finding the word laughable. "They provided information and photographs to the press. Mr. Chamberlain was not happy about it."

"Sounds like he needs a better class of friends!"

Adam nodded at her assessment. "I was delighted when he announced we would be returning to Florida. Some of his friends probably haven't noticed he's gone, although they'll get the picture when the chalet is sold."

Sierra's jaw dropped. "Sold?"

"Phoenix has made it clear that he doesn't want to go back there. Of course, it might be the depression doing the talking."

One could hope. Because if he didn't go back there, she had a sickening feeling he might stay here.

"How's his therapy going?" she asked, hoping for good news.

But that wasn't what she got.

"Slow." Adam sighed. "Since most days he doesn't want to do his exercises."

"That must make your job difficult."

"Oh, it does. And it feeds his frustration, as well, because he refuses to give up hope."

"Of walking without a cane?" Sierra inquired.

Adam nodded. "Walking without a cane…running…. skiing. He wants to be as good as before the accident."

"That's not likely to happen, is it?" she asked softly.

Adam cleared his throat. "I have already said too much, Miss Ramstad. I just wanted you to know why he is being a jerk."

"I understand. Thanks."

When Sierra returned to her bedroom, Phoenix's large suitcases were open on the foot of the bed.

"I'll need a bureau where I can put away his things. Hope you can accommodate me, Miss Ramstad."

Where Phoenix barked orders, his employees asked politely. She appreciated their manners.

"Sure." She grabbed a tote bag from the closet and started to fill it with her things. Over her shoulder, she called out, "I'll be out of your way in a few minutes."

"Oh, no rush, Miss Ramstad."

"Please, call me Sierra."

Adam smiled.

While she finished filling her bag with clothes, he hung an assortment of designer clothing in the closet. All of the garments screamed expensive and were far more formal than the t-shirt and shorts Adam had on. Did Phoenix plan to wear them? If so, when and where? Once again, she had an uneasy feeling that her employer was here for the long haul.

Phoenix Chamberlain was accustomed to a robust social life, if the press images were to be believed. Of course, that was before his car accident. Recently, the only time his photograph had graced the tabloids, his palms had been up, as if to ward off the swarming paparazzi, and he'd worn the same pain-induced grimace she'd seen firsthand.

Sierra finished clearing out the bureau and hastily grabbed a section of outfits from the closet, which she took to the adjacent room. Adam had finished unpacking his suitcase and was glancing around.

"Can I help you with something?" Sierra asked.

"I've got some equipment that I need to bring in for Mr. Chamberlain's sessions. I don't think you want it in the lobby."

He was right about that. "The resort has a gym on the main floor. There should be room in there for your equipment."

"Mr. Chamberlain has to have privacy."

Sierra nodded. She couldn't blame him for that. "If I have my treadmill moved to storage, will that be enough space?"

Adam squinted, as if visualizing the room sans the item she had mentioned. "Yes, I think that will work."

"Great! I'll call someone to move it."

"No need. Tommy and I can handle it."

"All right." That was settled. The invasion of her privacy was officially complete.

She forced a smile that was cut short by a snuffle coming from Phoenix. "Can the two of you skip the chitchat? I know that you have more things to do with your time than flirt!" he yelled.

Flirt? Sierra felt her face turn red, but it wasn't merely embarrassment that brought the heat rushing into her cheeks. The nerve of the man accusing her of flirting, as if spending a few minutes talking to a colleague meant she was interested in him. And to think minutes earlier she had started to feel sorry for Phoenix. Every ounce of empathy had evaporated now.

Adam nodded. "Sorry, Mr. Chamberlain," he mouthed.

Sierra nodded but she was too mad to say she was sorry.

While Adam and Tommy moved the treadmill to storage to make room for the physical therapy equipment, she changed the linens on the futon bed where she would sleep, gathered up her toiletries from the bathroom and put out clean towels. Then, satisfied that everything was in order, she turned to leave.

As Sierra entered the bedroom, she braced herself for an unpleasant exchange. But to her surprise, Phoenix was asleep on the sofa. His bad leg was propped on the coffee table, one of her colorful pillows under the heel serving as a cushion. In sleep he appeared less intimidating than he had while barking out orders. But even in slumber he wore a grimace that pulled at the corners of his mouth. Add a wheelchair and a cane, and it should have made him vulnerable. Only none of that did.

Nor did it take away from his overall good looks. With his chiseled cheekbones and square jaw, the man was handsome. No getting around that, even in his diminished physical state. Nor was there any getting around his reputation as a playboy. His polished looks and extensive bank account made him quite a catch.

Sierra tiptoed past him, eager to avoid further unpleasantness. At the door, she chanced a glance back. The less interaction she had with her boss, the better.

Phoenix woke to the sound of the door closing. He straightened on the sofa and turned his neck to one side and then the other. Yet another sore muscle for Adam to work on during their evening session. If Phoenix went. Perhaps he'd skip it again. It was this kind of thinking that made him angry, as it also left him feeling defeated. He wanted to get better, but what if he never did? What if the physicians were right?

Phoenix rose unsteadily to his feet, bearing as much of his weight as possible on the cane. He hated it. He hated that it shouted to the world that Phoenix Chamberlain was no longer the man he used to be.

But he had been right to come to Seaside Haven. He'd come here to find a purpose. Something, anything, to give his life meaning if it turned out that all of the physicians were right about his prognosis.

The best memories of his childhood were rooted here. The place had been his sanctuary, both during his grandfather's illness and after his death. Where his relationship with his parents had always been rocky, a young Phoenix had been the apple of his grandfather's eye.

He wondered what his grandfather would think if he could see Phoenix now. His bum leg wouldn't be an issue. But what had he done with his life. His grandfather had put his trust in Phoenix. He had left him his fortune and all of his real estate, not the least of which was the resort.

"Everything that I have will be yours someday." Phoenix could hear his grandfather's raspy voice as he'd made the promise. "I know you'll take good care of the resort, because you love it here as much as I do."

Guilt settled over Phoenix now like a thick blanket of fog. Yeah, he'd loved it so much he hadn't been back since his grandfather passed away. Thank God Sierra was so good at her job. She'd restored the aging resort and had brought in record profits as well. When all was said and done, Phoenix would see to it that she was properly compensated.

"Do you need anything, Mr. Chamberlain?" The question came from Adam, who with Tommy's help, was bringing in the weight bench Phoenix thought of as a torture device.

"I'm going to lie down for a little while," he replied bitterly.

Adam frowned at his reply. "Do you think that's a good idea, sir? Your muscles are probably stiff from the drive over, especially since we didn't get in a session this morning."

Adam was being diplomatic. His choice of wording made it sound as if the omission of the morning session had been an oversight rather than because Phoenix had refused to get out of bed.

"I'm going to lie down," Phoenix repeated, heading in the direction of the bed.

Adam shrugged his shoulders as if to say suit yourself.

Tommy cleared his throat. "As soon as we finish, I'm going to take off if that's okay with you sir?"

Tommy Wynn had worked for the Chamberlain's for a decade; more often Phoenix's designated driver than not. Sometimes he also stepped in the role of bouncer when party guests got out of control. There hadn't been much need for the latter the past few months since Phoenix's partying days were over.

"This mishap of yours might be for the best," his mother had said just that morning. "You have to grow up sometime Phoenix. You need to make sound investments for your future. God knows your father didn't learn that before it was too late."

"I'd say you made out well," he'd responded.

She'd pursed her lips at his sarcastic remark, causing fine lines to feather around her mouth. At fifty-five, Betty Chamberlain Faulk remained a beautiful woman thanks to the skills of an expensive plastic surgeon.

"I did what was necessary." All these years later, her second husband remained a source of friction between her and Phoenix.

He tried to block out the words his mother had said.

"Mr. Chamberlain?"

Phoenix glanced over his shoulder, realizing he'd never answered Tommy.

"Fine," he replied.

Tommy offered a jaunty salute. He always seemed to be in a good mood. Same for Adam. Phoenix used to be like that, too. He missed his old disposition as much as he missed his mobility.

"I assume Miss Ramstad cleared out her belongings."

Adam answered this time. "Yes sir, Sierra moved her things to the other room and I got all of your things put away."

Phoenix barely heard the last part of his reply. First name basis. For a reason he couldn't fathom, he didn't' like Adam's familiarity with her.

"The last time I saw her, she was on the phone in her office." Adam added before he and Tommy turned to walk away.

Draped in the frumpy red vinyl raincoat Sierra had fit his preconceived notion perfectly. But once she peeled it off and shoved the damp blond hair from her face, she wasn't at all what he'd expected. Phoenix found her attractive, which was a surprise in itself. She wasn't anything like the flashy women, whose beauty relied on a lot of enhancement including breast augmentation that usually caught his attention. Sierra was pretty in an understated way. What would she look like dressed up for a night on the town? He silently answered himself with a second question. *What did it matter?*

He looked around the room that had been his grandfather's. The bedding had been turned down; the lines that peeked from beneath the comforter were creased in places, leaving little doubt that someone had just changed the linens for him. He ran his fingers over the pillowcase. He would be sleeping in her bed. And she would be in the room next to his. He swallowed hard and told himself the sudden upswing in his pulse rate was only because he had a lot to learn from the efficient Miss Ramstad if he hoped to operate the resort as capably as she had been.

Phoenix was done shirking all responsibility. Life as he'd known it was over in more ways than one. In the meantime, he had an appointment with an orthopedic surgeon the following week. He hoped to receive a better prognosis than the one the previous physicians had given him.

As if on cue, his leg muscles began to cramp and spasm. He leaned on the door frame to the bathroom to take the weight off of his left leg. When he glanced up, he spotted the words *Non-habit forming* written in red lipstick on the mirror, accompanied by a bottle of over-the-counter pain pills on the counter.

He studied his reflection in the mirror. The dark circles under his eyes and gaunt cheeks no longer took him by surprise. But it came as a jolt to realize he was smiling.

Chapter Three

A couple of hours later, Sierra was in the resort's galley-style kitchen helping the chef with dinner preparations when the swinging doors opened up and her unwanted guest lumbered inside.

Chef Bijon Invar looked up from the pot of soup he was stirring on the stovetop.

"Sorry, but guests aren't allowed in the kitchen," the chef said politely, but firmly in his thick accent.

The kitchen was Bijon's domain, and he didn't care for guests breaching its doors. To call him temperamental would be putting it mildly. But he was a good chef, with over twenty years of experience operating some of the finest restaurants in New York. Sierra considered it a major coup that she'd managed to hire Bijon on as the head chef.

Phoenix's brow raised in surprise. It was a good bet that he wasn't used to being told where he could and could not go, especially on property that he owned.

Hoping to ward off a battle of the egos, Sierra chimed in, "I think we can make an exception for this guest since he signs our paychecks."

"Mister Chamberlain?" the chef quizzed, his tone brimming with disbelief. His gaze shifted to his cane. "I didn't recognize you…"

Bijon was known for his innovative dishes but not so much for his tact. Sierra decided she would make the introduction.

"Mr. Chamberlain, this is Bijon Invar, the resort's chef. You're in for a treat at dinner. He is making his specialty, pan-seared grouper in an herbed butter sauce."

"Sounds delicious." He acknowledged the chef with a perfunctory nod, but his gaze strayed to Sierra and his eyes narrowed. "And why are *you* wearing an apron?"

"I'm just lending a hand with prep. Nothing that requires a culinary degree."

Eyes still narrowed, Phoenix asked, "Do you help out often, Miss Ramstad?"

His questioned seemed rooted in curiosity, rather than genuine concern.

"I wouldn't say often, but I do what is needed, whether that's here in the kitchen or someplace else at the resort."

Indeed, during her tenure as manager, Sierra had changed soiled linens and a dozen other less-than-glamourous jobs. She figured her willingness to roll up her sleeves was why she had earned the staff's respect.

Phoenix rubbed his chin. "I see."

Unfortunately, Sierra couldn't tell from his expression whether he thought this was a good use of her managerial skills or not. Squaring her shoulders, she asked, "Was there something you needed, Mr. Chamberlain?"

"No. Just taking a look around as so much has changed." From his tone, she couldn't tell if he was happy about that or feeling nostalgic for the past.

Speaking of changes, Phoenix had undergone a bit of transformation as well. His black hair was wet as if he'd recently showered. He wore it combed back from his forehead but a few curls fell across his brow. His face was shaved, all shadow gone from his angular jawline. But it wasn't the absence of the stubble that caught her attention. It was the absence of a grimace.

"I see you took me up on my offer."

The faintest smile lurked on his lips when he asked, "How do you know?"

"Well, you look…rested."

Despite his obvious weight loss, the man was definitely handsome. He had on a crisp white shirt that was tucked into a pair of khaki dress pants. The carved wooden cane in his hand added to his air of sophistication.

"I got in a nap," he announced.

"And a therapy session?" Sierra quizzed.

"No, I was trying to relieve some of the pain. Don't let Adam's baby face fool you. He can be brutal."

Phoenix's subtle attempt at humor came as a nice surprise. She decided to return it.

"They say no pain, no gain."

Just that quickly, his expression changed. She gave an inaudible sigh. Apparently she had reminded him of his slow recovery. While he looked away, Sierra and Bijon traded covert shrugs. Breaking the silence, Phoenix asked, "New ovens?"

"Yes. Last summer."

He glanced around, nodding in approval.

Since it was much easier to talk about business than to exchange pleasantries, Sierra continued. "The walk-in freezer just needed some repairs and it was good as new."

"Excellent." Phoenix nodded, but she got the impression he wasn't listening to what she said.

"Are you hungry? Dinner won't be served for another hour, but…"

He interrupted her. "That's alright. Adam made me an omelet." He sent her a smile that bordered on sheepish. "And he was disappointed that your bread wasn't whole wheat."

"Oh?" Sierra wasn't sure how she felt about guests rummaging through the cupboards. She smiled thinly. "Bijon and I will be going out tomorrow for groceries and supplies for the resort. If you give me a list, I'll be happy to pick up whatever you need."

"I'll have Adam put something together." Phoenix's lip curled. "He likes for me to eat healthy."

"The body is a temple," she chimed.

He snorted. "Mine feels more like an ancient ruin."

Phoenix looked to the far side of the room and his scowl returned to his face. Sierra followed the line of his vision to Bijon's calendar with the days that had passed marked off with red Xs.

"Is something wrong?" she asked.

He shook his head, and without another word, turned and limped out of the kitchen.

"Real friendly, isn't he," Bijon muttered sarcastically.

Sierra picked up her knife and returned her attention to the vegetables on the cutting board. "He'll be gone before we know it and things will be back to normal." At least she hoped that would be the case.

Seeing the days marked off the calendar and realizing that three months had passed since the accident spoiled Phoenix's mood. The ibuprofen Sierra had given him had taken the edge off his physical pain. His emotional pain, however, was another matter.

Phoenix wished the storm would subside so that he could sit on the deck and watch the waves rise and fall. The ocean had always had a calming effect on his emotions. Even on days such as this one, the waves crashed ruthlessly against the shore, but the water always receded and eventually calmed. Soon enough, the sun would come out and chase away the gloom, and the beach would be the same as it had been before the storm. Nothing about his life was predictable, except for his bad leg and the pain that came with it.

Phoenix realized how much he missed his grandfather. Phoenix Chamberlain, Sr., had been the only loving adult in the young Phoenix's life. After his father's death, his mother had remarried, and Phoenix had been shunted aside. Even now Phoenix refused to consider how desperate his mother must have felt to find her financial stability stripped from her. During his last visit to the resort, as they'd sat in this very room, his grandfather had told him, "I don't condone the way your mother has treated you since remarrying, but try to see things from her perspective."

"What do you mean?" he'd asked.

His grandfather had laid his wrinkled hand on Phoenix's shoulder.

"I loved your dad dearly, but I'm not blind to his shortcomings. He made some poor choices over the years. Choices that your mother has had to deal with."

"What are you saying?"

"I'm saying, make me proud, Phoenix."

A final request that Phoenix had failed to honor.

"Mr. Chamberlain?" Adam poked his head around the door.

Although Phoenix was awake, he kept his eyes closed and feigned sleep. He'd been lying on the bed in his room reminiscing and trying to work out the details of his plan. A plan that Sierra wasn't going to like when he eventually told her about it.

His grandfather had left Phoenix the resort with the expectations he would actually run it, rather than sign checks and authorize purchases when he took a break from the ski slopes.

"Mr. Chamberlain?" Adam called again.

Leave me alone! Phoenix shouted the words to himself but didn't say them out loud. He was tired of being sullen and contrary, even as he felt powerless to change his mood. So he kept his eyes closed and his breathing deep and even. He expected that Adam would go away and Phoenix would continue to sulk in silence.

But his physical therapist wasn't alone.

"He's sleeping soundly," Phoenix heard Adam whisper to whoever was with him. "Just go in and get what you need."

"I'd hate to disturb him." Sierra replied.

Once again Phoenix found himself wanting to shout, *leave me alone!* His reason this time was embarrassment. When he'd returned to his room, he'd shucked off his other clothes and now lay atop the comforter wearing a pair of navy nylon shorts. He was shirtless and his pale frame was an imitation of the tanned, physically fit man he'd been. Still, it would be the lesser of two evils, if Sierra's gaze remained on his chest and didn't deviate to the web of scars on his leg.

"Perhaps I should come back later," she said.

"You'd rather see him when he's awake?" Adam's tone was wry and teasing.

Sierra laughed and Phoenix bristled inwardly. Her laughter with the younger man grated his nerves.

"That's a good point," she said.

Footsteps sounded then. Was Adam leaving? Where was Sierra? Phoenix listened for the creak of the floor or the rustle of fabric, anything to announce that she was inside the room. Finally, he heard a door squeak. He chanced opening his eyes. Sierra was in the walk-in closet, standing under the light. He studied her figure as she rose up on her toes, stretching to fetch something from one of the shelves. After she had whatever it was that she'd come in to get, Phoenix watched her turn off the light and gently close the closet door.

She tiptoed toward the bedroom door, but then stopped at the foot of the bed. If she would have looked at his face, she would have realized he was awake. But she wasn't looking at his face. She was studying his leg. The calf was noticeably smaller that its counterpart on his right leg. Adam attributed the disparity to muscle atrophy, although he couldn't guarantee Phoenix that regular exercise would fix that.

Her gaze wandered up to his knee before skimming his thigh. She gaped at the jagged scars where bone had ripped through his flesh and multiple surgeries had followed. She closed her eyes briefly. Did he disgust her? Did she pity him? He wasn't sure which reaction would be worse. He only knew he couldn't tolerate anymore of her examination.

"Have you seen enough?"

Sierra nearly dropped the scarf she'd retrieved from the closet.

"You scared me!"

Looking for a confrontation, he propped up on one elbow. "You didn't answer my question, Miss Ramstad."

"I didn't mean to stare. I was just…"

She cleared her throat. Even in the dim light, he could see that she was flustered and probably embarrassed. But definitely not aroused. Why would she be? He was repulsive. Angrily he spat out in a suggestive tone, "My leg might not be in working order, but I assure you that everything else is."

She dropped the scarf, and her hand flew to her face. "Excuse me?"

"You heard me."

At that, he expected her to stomp out of the room in a huff. He should've known his smart and sassy resort manager would do no such thing. Instead, Sierra drew closer to his side of the bed.

"I heard you. I was trying to give you the benefit of the doubt."

"And you expect me to apologize?" he said, keeping his tone brazen.

"Well, as a matter of fact I do." She fisted her hands but let them rest on her hips and sent him a convex stare.

Given Phoenix's position on the bed, he admired her rounded hips and firm backside causing parts of his body that had been dormant for too long to awaken. Some of the frustration and anger dissipated, only to be replaced by feelings that were far more dangerous. Even though Phoenix knew he was playing with fire he couldn't keep his eyes from traveling up Sierra's slender frame and lingering on all of the parts that interested him.

"Well?" she demanded.

Their eyes met. Collided was more like it. Phoenix didn't see sparks fly but he felt them as they showered his bare skin. The sensation was one he had never felt and he reveled in it. Afraid he may never feel this way again.

"You first," he taunted.

"You expect *me* to apologize to you?" Her tone hovered between incredulous and infuriated. Perversely, he found it sexy. As he did her narrowed eyes and pursed lips.

"That's right."

"What am I to apologize for?" she quizzed.

"Well, you're in my room...uninvited. *A matter that could be remedied easily enough*, his libido whispered before he could quiet it.

"This is...well, *was* my bedroom."

"Technically, as the resort's owner..."

She stopped him there and talked over his clarification of the room's ownership.

"I just came in to get a scarf from the closet. I would have asked permission, her lips twisted on the word, but you were sleeping and I didn't want to disturb you. If you want an apology for that, then, I'm sorry for the inconvenience, Mr. Chamberlain."

She didn't sound sorry. She sounded agitated and ready to combust. Phoenix knew he should stop provoking her, but he couldn't help himself.

"You got your scarf, yet here you are, Sierra! Under the circumstances I think we should be on a first-name basis. Agree?"

"I...I..." she stuttered, glaring at him.

"You were staring at me. Or maybe I should say gawking. The way one does a train wreck."

"I wasn't staring," she insisted.

Phoenix pushed himself up to a sitting position. In doing so, excruciating pain radiated from his knee, shooting down to his ankle. He wasn't able to bite back his yelp. Apparently, the ibuprofen had worn off.

"Mr. Chamberlain?" she started forward.

"Phoenix, call me Phoenix!" he spat in anger. In that instant, he was back to being angry with himself and everyone else. "Just go."

She turned on her heel and walked out of the room with her shoulders squared and her chin up.

Phoenix flopped back on the bed. His anger dissipated and shame settled in its place. He wondered what it said about him that the most alive he'd felt in months had been while provoking an employee. Sierra was right. He was the one who owed her an apology.

Sierra was enraged. She stomped out of the resort without saying a word to anyone. *Phoenix Chamberlain.* Who did he think he was? She didn't care if he owned Seaside Haven. The man was acting like an inconsiderate tyrant. One with a faulty memory to boot.

He'd agreed with her plan to turn the manager's apartment into a luxurious suite for high-end guests. He'd agreed to let her stay in the unused owner's suite. She had saved their written correspondence to that effect. Maybe she should remind him. Maybe she should return to his room and confront him.

She swallowed, recalling the sight of the man lying on her bed. Maybe she had stared for a couple of minutes longer than was polite. But Phoenix Chamberlain sans shirt and wearing shorts had certainly caught her attention. And since she thought he was asleep, she'd figured she would get a closer look.

She'd gotten an eyeful, all right. The accident had taken a toll on his once-fit body and he was thinner than he'd appeared when fully dressed. Regardless, he was all male, and seeing him spread out on her bed had an unsettling effect on her thinking. And on her breathing.

Sierra tried to recall how long it had been since a man had stirred the air in her lungs. Or that sensation of butterflies in her stomach. She couldn't. Within the first year of her marriage with Turner, things had gone from acceptable to bad. From there, they'd made the leap to awful. In all, three years of her life wasted. It still shamed her to think that she'd allowed herself to be abused for that length of time.

In the immediate aftermath of her ugly divorce, she'd been too shell-shocked to think of dating again. Once she'd moved to Seaside and landed the job at the resort, she'd been happy to focus on her career. It wasn't that she didn't have time for dating. She didn't make time. While staring at Phoenix, Sierra had begun to have second thoughts.

It was after midnight when she finally returned to the resort. Standing in the kitchen now, she rubbed her temples. Adam had the blender on high, making it easy for her to wave and go. But he eyed her knowingly. "What's got you so upset?"

"Not what. Who!"

"I think I can guess who you mean," Adam said, pulling Sierra from her introspection.

Be that as it may, Sierra didn't gossip, much less talk disrespectfully about her boss, so she worked up what she hoped passed for a smile. "I'm just frustrated with one of our suppliers," she said. "He keeps jacking up the prices."

"Supplier, hmm?" Adam didn't look fooled.

Sierra cleared her throat. "I'll just get out of your way. Goodnight."

Chapter Four

Phoenix slept poorly, tossing and turning for the better part of the night. His conscience bothered him as much as his leg. He'd heard Sierra come in, her steps light as she entered the adjacent room. He'd imagined her curled up on the uncomfortable futon, and his conscience nipped at him again. Not because he'd displaced her from her bed, but because his imagination had lingered on what she'd been wearing.

He tossed the covers back. He needed to apologize to her. He'd leave out the part about his wayward imagination and concentrate on his rude behavior from the day before.

He found Sierra on the private deck of the resort. She was seated in one of the lounge chairs, her bible in her lap. A cup of coffee was on a small table next to her. Adam was at the rail drinking a green concoction through a straw. He spotted Phoenix through the sliding glass door and rushed over to open it.

"Good morning, Mr. Chamberlain!" he exclaimed with his usual good cheer. "You're up early. Sierra and I were just enjoying the sunrise."

The man's enthusiasm should have been contagious. Phoenix glanced at Sierra, who looked as unmotivated as he felt.

"Can I get you a smoothie?"

What Phoenix wanted was a cup of high-octane coffee and a couple extra-strength ibuprofen. But what he needed was a few minutes alone with Sierra, and Adam had just provided him the perfect excuse.

"Yes, Adam. A smoothie would be great. Thanks."

Phoenix's response not only had Adam's eyes widening; Sierra stopped reading and turned to look at him.

"You're always pushing about their health benefits," Phoenix added.

"I didn't think you were listening," the younger man replied with comical honesty.

"I'll also take a cup of coffee and a couple ibuprofen when you get a chance."

Adam grinned. "Coming right up. Do you need anything, Sierra?"

She shook her head. "No thanks."

Once they were alone, Phoenix moved to the lounge chair next to hers. Bearing his weight on the cane, he tried to lower himself slowly, but his knee gave out halfway down and he landed on the seat with a plop. He grunted and surprised them both by admitting, "It's so depressing to need assistance taking a seat."

She studied him for a moment before nodding in agreement. Then she went back to her bible.

He tried again. "It's a nice morning. The calm after the storm."

She nodded again, this time without looking up. It was not even six am and Sierra was showered, dressed and on the deck. Most of the women he knew would have been asleep after a late night of partying.

Phoenix cleared his throat, but the words still stuck before finally coming out. "I…I owe you an apology for how I acted yesterday."

"Yes. You do." Her tone was straightforward.

Phoenix rubbed a hand over the stubble on his jaw. "Could you maybe stop reading for a minute and look at me?"

She read a few more words, exhaled slowly and then closed the book. Turning in her seat, she gave him her full attention. He almost wished she hadn't. Big green eyes fringed with amazingly long lashes left him feeling vulnerable.

"I am sorry…the things I said…I was out of line."

"Apology accepted." She lifted her hand and ran her fingers through her hair in a gesture that struck him as almost tentative. "I should have waited to get my scarf."

"You left it on the floor, by the way."

"I know."

He reached into the pocket of his robe and pulled out the crumpled piece of fabric. "Here you go."

A smile tugged at her lips. "Thanks."

"We got off on the wrong foot." He snorted at his unintentionally apropos phrasing. Since humbling himself wasn't as difficult as he'd presumed it to be, he continued, "I should have realized that my early arrival here would cause some chaos."

"Can I ask you something?" she said after a moment.

"Sure."

"Did you even read the monthly reports?" Her tone held a note of censure. The woman certainly didn't pull any punches.

"No. I glanced at them." He decided he owed her the truth. "Well, some of them."

His stomach took a surprising roll. It had been a long time since Phoenix had cared what someone thought of him. Not since his grandfather.

"I should have read them." A responsible owner would have, he admitted to himself. "But I did and still do trust you and your judgment. Besides, we graduated from the same college."

"*You* have a degree?"

The shock on her face was unmistakable and reflected in the disbelief in her tone. Phoenix's battered ego took yet another blow.

"I haven't put it to use, but yes, I have a degree, earned a few years before you would have started classes. When I interviewed you for the job – which he'd done by phone between runs down the Swiss Alps – I was impressed by your credentials, even though you didn't have much experience."

Her expression turned oddly guarded and she looked away.

"I got married right after graduation." She paused. "My husband didn't think I needed to work."

"You're married?" That came as a surprise. An unpleasant one based on the way his stomach churned. Phoenix rallied as quickly as he could, hoping that none of his dismay showed in his expression. Her marital status was none of his business, legally or otherwise.

"Happily divorced," she replied. Her jaw clenched after she said it and she reached for her cup of coffee.

He couldn't help but be intrigued. Not only about what had happened to end Sierra's marriage, but what kind of man would have let her go. But he kept his questions to himself. Business was the basis of their relationship. And when it came to business, in spite of the degree he'd earned, Phoenix had a lot to learn.

Sierra was no longer clenching her jaw. In fact, he heard excitement in her voice and saw a spark in her eyes as she told him, "I saw so much potential for change the first time I toured the resort. The oceanfront view is amazing." She motioned to the horizon where the sun blazed gold and orange before blurring into shades of pink.

"The resort should have been booked year-round. Yet it had vacancies during the peak tourist seasons. And the internet reviews were dismal. People want amenities when they go on vacation. Give them what they want and they'll come back again."

"I may not have read every one of your reports, but that much I figured out."

"I would imagine the bottom line speaks for itself," she said dryly.

He nodded. "It speaks volumes." Revenues were up and the money he'd invested in upgrades would be repaid in no time. His future was secure, financially at least.

And he owed it all to Sierra.

Guilt throbbed like a bad tooth since his new plan would see her displaced from her job. But he doubted someone of Sierra's caliber would want to stay on, basically sharing managerial duties with him. He'd offer her the option, of course. As much as he wanted to run the resort, he didn't plan to work seven days a week like she apparently did.

If she left, more likely when, he would see to it that she was nicely compensated. He made a mental note to meet with his attorney to draft up a generous severance package when he went into Atlanta for his doctor appointment.

"Thank you," he told her now.

Then he reached over and laid one of his hands over hers. The gesture was intended to be companionable, but the way his body responded to the benign contact was far immoral in nature.

She pulled her hand away, using it to tuck a few strands of hair behind her ear. Her cheeks had turned a becoming shade of pink, and he couldn't help wondering if it was the contact that had thrown her or his gratitude.

Finally, she replied, "The year-end bonus I received was thanks enough." She picked up her coffee cup then and focused her attention on its contents. "I like living here at the resort. And I love my job. I'm good at what I do."

He found the last comment odd. She seemed to be trying to convince him of her competence. If so, she needn't have bothered.

While he covertly studied Sierra's profile, she sipped her coffee and gazed at the horizon. He took in the slope of her nose and her delicate jaw that ended in a perfectly rounded chin. Her beauty stirred him in a way he found both compelling and concerning. The squawk of seagulls and slap of waves on the sand were the only sounds to break the silence until the door opened and Adam stepped out onto the deck. He carried a tray that held a cup of coffee and a glass filled with a green concoction.

"Here you go, Mr. C. One smoothie as requested. I took the liberty of adding a banana." The young man grinned. "They're an excellent source of potassium."

"Yum." Phoenix grimaced. He hated bananas as much as he hated smoothies.

"Well, I need to meet Bijon to go shopping. I have your list," Sierra told Adam. Then she rose to her feet, book in her hand, her gaze fixed on Phoenix. "Enjoy your smoothie."

Was it his imagination or was she biting back a smile?

Chapter Five

Since his arrival at Seaside Haven, Phoenix had been up each day by dawn. He'd felt more rested the past few days than he had during the past several years. This morning he couldn't claim to feel the same. Phoenix had slept sporadically when he'd slept at all. That was because his appointment with the doctor was today. He didn't want to believe that nothing more could be done when it came to his recovery but it was a good possibility that this physician would tell him the same thing all of the other physicians had. The same stifling sense of defeat that had defined his life for the past three months settled over him.

After lying in bed, his mind racing as much as it was wandering, he finally threw back the covers and struggled out of bed. His leg was stiff. It always was first thing in the morning. He performed a couple of the stretching exercises Adam recommended and then got dressed in his usual attire of khaki pants and a light-weight-shirt.

As he passed the adjacent room, he noticed that the door was ajar. He glanced inside, doubting as he did so that he would find Sierra there.

At this hour, she would be out on the deck, a cup of coffee on the table at her side and the bible on her lap. It was how she started her days unless the weather was bad. So, for the past week, coffee on the deck was how Phoenix had started his days as well.

Movement inside of the room caught his attention. Not only was Sierra there, she was undressing. He should look away. But he couldn't. He stood rooted in place, gaze fixated on her slim body. Her movements were practical, hardly choreographed to seduce. Still, the sight of her smooth skin and lean contours made it difficult to breathe.

He managed to inhale, and a familiar and all too pleasing aroma filled his nostrils. Clean and crisp with a hint of floral. It was the same fragrance that teased him at night while he lay in her bed. The sheets may have been fresh, but her scent was all around the room. Making him yearn. The heat enveloped him now. He took a couple of steps backward and cleared his throat noisily in an effort to announce his presence. When he drew even with the door a second time, Sierra was pulling it open.

"Good morning, Phoenix," she said.

"Good morning."

She'd exchanged the blue shirt she usually wore for a lighter version with the resort's logo embroidered on the chest and he found himself staring at her breasts. He ripped his gaze away only to have it settle on the tangled sheets that littered the futon bed behind her. He frowned.

"That doesn't look very comfortable," he murmured.

Sierra glanced over her shoulder. "Probably not as comfortable as the pillow top mattress you're sleeping on," she agreed. "But it's not bad."

He grimaced. "I'm sorry for the inconvenience my stay has caused you."

Her eyes widened fractionally, but that was the only indication his words surprised her. She nodded. "It's okay."

He changed the subject. "I thought you'd be out on the deck."

"I was, but I spilled coffee on my shirt."

"So, that's why you changed it." He realized his faux pas even before her eyes narrowed.

"How long have you been up?" she asked.

"Up?" he shrugged, surprised by her question.

"You know, awake? You have a doctor's appointment today, right?"

Her gazed lowered to the cane gripped in his hand. "Right." *And an appointment with his attorney,* Phoenix added silently.

"I'll say a prayer for you."

"Thanks." He frowned at the cane. "I'm hoping for a more promising prognosis."

"And if you don't get it? What then?"

Phoenix took a deep breath and exhaled slowly. "To be honest with you, I don't know what I'll do. At what point do

I just…give up." His fingers tightened on the cane's handle until his knuckles turned white.

"You can't expect to fully recover if you don't put in the effort."

He made a scoffing noise. No one had dared say such a thing to him. Even Adam trod lightly when it came to admonishing Phoenix for his lack of effort.

Instead of telling her to go to hell, he replied with similar honesty. "Some days everything seems so…pointless."

The admission hung between them, suspended in the ensuing silence. Something flickered in her eyes. Was it understanding? Empathy?

"That is depression doing the talking," she said after a moment. Her tone was filled with compassion, which only made it worse.

Since he was already feeling helpless, his pride made him retort, "What are you a psychiatrist now?"

She appeared to take his irritable tone in stride. "No. I just know that when a person is at his or her lowest point, it's not always easy to get back up."

"Sounds as if you're speaking from experience?"

She eyed him for a moment before speaking again.

"I'm heading back out to the deck. I have a few more emails to reply to before I get to work. Are you coming?"

Her switch in topics made it clear she knew something about how difficult it was to climb one's way back up after hitting the bottom. Her divorce seemed the obvious culprit so he let the matter drop.

"Can I get you a cup of coffee? I'll even carry it for you," she offered with a smile that seemed more flirtatious than merely friendly. He decided to think of that as progress.

Phoenix followed her. His pace was slow and measured compared to her brisk one, and far less graceful. The view was well worth it, he thought, as his gaze dipped south to watch her hips swing side to side. His interest was piqued again.

"Is Adam out on the deck already?" he asked.

"No. He went for a run on the beach but he should be back within the hour. I'm sure he'll be happy to make you one of those smoothies then."

Phoenix groaned.

She stopped at the granite topped island in the kitchen and poured coffee before starting for the door that led to the deck.

It was breezier this morning than it had been on previous days. The wind caught her hair and pushed several strands of it across her face. She finger-combed them back after sitting their coffee on a table and settling onto her lounge chair. His fingers itched to touch her hair. To touch her.

By the time Phoenix had his legs stretched out in front of him; Sierra was already tapping on the computer's keyboard. While he appreciated her above-and-beyond the call of duty approach, it wasn't expected. Nor was it particularly healthy. He nearly chuckled aloud at that thought. As if he had any right to judge another person's lifestyle.

He glanced idly at the computer screen, expecting to see her replying to business-related emails or confirming reservations.

"Do you always read other people's correspondence?" she inquired blandly.

"No…sorry. I assumed that whatever you were writing was business-related."

"I do have a life, you know," she said as if trying to convince him.

Not much of one he thought but kept his opinion to himself. He did ask, "Who is Ryan?"

Her former husband? Her lover?

She gave him her full attention, cat-green eyes blazing with an emotion he couldn't pinpoint. "She is my niece," she answered.

"Lucky you." When she frowned, he added, "I am an only child. No siblings, no nieces or nephews. Just me."

With his father and grandfather deceased and his mother estranged, that was the case.

"I have a twin sister, Sienna." Her expression softened, and a smile lurked around the corners of her mouth.

"Are you two close?"

"Yes." Now she frowned again. "Well, not as close as I'd like. My brother-in-law, Del, was a police officer…he was killed in the line of duty. It's taken a toll on my sister."

"God, I'm sorry, Sierra," Phoenix said, although the words seemed inadequate under the circumstances. In some ways it made his own struggles seem minor, especially since his accident had been the result of aggressive paparazzi side-swiping the car he was riding in rather than something as honorable as protecting and serving others. It was a humbling realization.

"Ryan is five now. For the past couple of summers, she and my sister have come to Seaside over the Fourth of July holiday."

"So they'll be coming this summer?" he asked, oddly envious of the picture of domestic bliss that her words had conjured up.

"They stay with me, Phoenix. And there's no room at the resort," she replied.

It took him a moment to realize what she meant. He was staying in *her* room.

"Don't worry about it. What's done is done. I promised Ryan that she and her mom can come another time, maybe during Christmas."

The assumption being that Phoenix wouldn't be at Seaside Haven then. He swallowed. He wasn't planning on going anywhere.

While she went back to typing, he skimmed their surroundings. White-capped waves danced on the horizon before crashing to shore. Down the beach, he spotted Adam. He was a physically fit young man and Phoenix envied him.

"Are you a runner?" he asked Sierra, as he pointed in the direction of his physical therapist.

"No," she replied. "Running is hard on the knees. That's why I walk on the beach. Besides, I am a seashell addict."

He recalled the assortment of glass containers of various shapes and sizes nestled around the lobby and in her bedroom and bath. Some people paid an interior decorator to bring in such touches, but Sierra had collected them herself.

"Do they have a twelve-step program for seashell addicts?"

She laughed. "I can't believe you actually made a joke."

He blinked. "I used to have a good sense of humor."

"Did you break that in the car accident, too?"

He laughed aloud, a raspy sound that scraped his throat as it came out.

"You're funny!"

Sierra closed her computer and rose to her feet just as Adam jogged up the steps that led from the beach. "Enjoy your run?" she asked as she sent Phoenix a wink.

"Y-yeah! Great…morning…for it," Adam replied, breathing heavily. "Hope you get a good report at your doctor's appointment," he added, having fully caught his breath. "I'm going inside for a shower."

Adam's comment brought back Phoenix's anxiety about seeing the specialist and his attorney in Atlanta. He rubbed his thigh. The daily regimen of ibuprofen had dulled the pain, but nothing was successful in taking it away completely.

"Are you afraid?" Sierra asked.

He shook his head as if to say no, but answered, "A little."

He swung his legs over the side of lounge chair and grabbed the railing, using his upper body strength, he levered to his feet. The breeze picked up, whipping several strands of blonde hair across Sierra's face. This time, Phoenix gave in to impulse and tucked it behind her ear before she could. Afterward, his hand lingered to her check. It was as soft as silk, just as he'd imagined.

He watched her eyes widen in surprise or interest. He needed to believe it was the latter. He needed to believe that *she* found him desirable. He caressed her check and her lips parted ever so slightly, and Phoenix leaned in for a kiss. When she didn't resist, he went back for more.

He settled his mouth firmly over hers this time. She rose on her tiptoe and tilted her head to one side. Without breaking off their kiss, she dropped the laptop onto the lounge chair's cushion. Both of her hands were free now, and she brought them up to his shoulders.

Raw and unrestrained passion coursed through Phoenix's veins. For the first time in months, he felt alive again. He kept one hand on the rail for support. But something told him that even if both of his legs had been in working order, his knees would have felt weak.

Sierra pulled back slowly, blinking up at him as if in disbelief. Although her hands remained on his shoulders, the moment was ending. He traced her lips with the pad of his thumb and felt her quiver.

"Phoenix, I don't think…" Her voice was barely above a whisper. He leaned closer to her and she shook her head. She dropped her arms to her sides and backed up a step. Then, turned and hurried inside, leaving him alone on the deck.

Chapter Six

Phoenix wanted to throw his cane across the doctor's office or plow his fist into the doctor's face, as if it were somehow the man's fault that Phoenix's leg was shattered beyond repair.

"You need to accept that your life has changed," the doctor was saying. "You need to find new hobbies, Mr. Chamberlain." The doctor cleared his throat, and then added, "I also recommend therapy."

"I'm in therapy!" Phoenix spat out.

"I'm not talking about physical therapy," the doctor announced, his expression kind and condescending. Phoenix balled his hands into fists in his lap in an attempt to keep from punching a hole in the wall. He stayed that way for the remainder of the appointment.

"I'm sorry, Mr. C," Tommy began as they left the doctor's office. "I know you were hoping for better news."

Phoenix didn't answer. Once they were in the Escalade, he barked an address at Tommy. At least his attorney wouldn't be able to contradict Phoenix's plans for his future. With so much else beyond his control, he needed to be in charge of something and the resort was all he had left.

Sierra had remained at the desk in her office for most of the day. She was still mentally berating herself for kissing Phoenix when she heard footsteps in the hall outside of her office. One set was uneven and accompanied by the distinctive click of a cane on the tile. The other was heavier. Phoenix and Tommy had returned from the doctor appointment.

Sierra exhaled through her mouth, then rose to her feet. On her way to the door, she smoothed her hair and schooled her expression into one of polite concern.

"How did the...?"

That was all she got out before Tommy shook his head.

Meanwhile, Phoenix never even glanced her way. He glared straight ahead with his jaw clenched, his dark eyebrows pinched in a scowl reminiscent of the expression he'd been wearing the first time they met. Whatever the physician had said, it hadn't been good news. Her heart sank. This, she knew, was Phoenix's worst fear.

That evening, Phoenix requested to have dinner in his room. Sierra had prepared the tray herself while Adam was creating some kind of smoothie. "Just leave the tray on the counter and I'll take it when I finish with this," he said as he added slices of banana to the blender. She nodded. The less interaction with Phoenix the better. For both of them.

She raised her voice so that Adam could hear. "So, bad news today?'

Adam stopped the blender and sighed. "Not necessarily bad news. Just not what he wanted to hear. He won't be skiing down the slopes again. And he's probably never going to walk without a limp and a cane. The faster he accepts that and moves on with his life, the better off he's going to be." He resumed the blender, rendering conversation impossible.

Sierra's heart had ached for Phoenix. But she stopped feeling sorry for him when, a week later, he remained in his room with the curtains drawn. Adam had been the only person allowed to enter, and then only to bring his meals.

At first, she'd been relieved that Phoenix hadn't joined her for coffee on the deck in the mornings. After that kiss they'd shared, things between them were bound to be awkward. But now, five days after his doctor appointment, she was out of both empathy and patience.

"You didn't have to take dinner to Phoenix?" she quizzed Adam.

"I am heading to the dining room to eat and I will take dinner to him when I have finished." He glanced at his watch. "It's early for your evening walk. It hasn't cooled off much outside yet."

Indeed, it was still hot, which is why she usually waited until late evening to walk on the beach. It was mostly empty by then, even the hardcore sunbathers having packed up for the day. "I know, but there's no new guests arriving and the dinner crowd was light because of the festival happening in town."

She inclined her head down the hallway. "Has he been out of his room today?"

"No, never even got out of bed." Adam shook his head. "He's going to be extra sore once he decides to rejoin the land of the living and resumes physical therapy."

Sierra pursed her lips and shook her head.

"I know what you're thinking," Adam said.

"That he's not only feeling sorry for himself but also sabotaging his recovery? When Adam didn't reply, Sierra demanded, "Well, am I wrong?"

"Not in the least."

This reply didn't come from Adam. It came from Phoenix, who was standing in the hallway, just outside the door to his room.

She swallowed hard. "I'm sorry."

"Oh, please. Don't ruin your frankness with an apology," he told Sierra as he trudged toward her. "Your honesty is one of the qualities I like about you."

He was looking for a fight, and she wouldn't disappoint him. She lifted her head, squaring her chin. "You're right. I'm not sorry. What I am is disappointed!"

Phoenix's dark brow elevated in surprise at that. "Disappointed?" he repeated.

Adam picked that moment to mumble something about having dinner before he walked away. Phoenix waited until the door closed behind him before he continued. "Well, you can get in line behind my mother! I've never been able to please her either." He shook his head and some of the rage went out of him. "Didn't Adam tell you? This is it Sierra! What you see is what you get!"

The comment momentarily caught Sierra off guard. But she chose not to dwell on his last statement. Instead, she remained focused on the subject at hand; his reaction to the physician's prognosis. Taking a step closer to him, she said, "You're not going to be able to ski the slopes in Europe again, or run a marathon. Even ballroom dancing may be out of the question."

Phoenix's voice thundered through the resort. "I don't need you to remind me of all the things I can no longer do!" The mocking smile he sent her vanished when he lost his balance. He was able to catch himself on the nearby door frame, but in doing so he had let go of the cane. The gold-tipped walking aid clattered to the floor and vicious cursing followed.

Sierra allowed him to vent his frustration, waiting until he was done to retrieve the cane and hold it out to him. He snatched it from her grip. She needed to make Phoenix use his anger to his advantage. Channeled correctly, it could prove to be beneficial. God knew she'd used her own anger as a catalyst for change.

So she went on to say, "Well, let me tell you what you can do. You can continue to be a resentful invalid or you can do something about it." She expected her words to get a rise out of him but to her consternation; the fight went out of

Phoenix. His voice lost its hostile edge and he stated, "But I am a bitter invalid."

"Adam said that you would get stronger if you wouldn't skip therapy for days at a time and put in minimal effort when you do it."

"So, you and Adam are discussing my therapy? I wasn't aware that the two of you had gotten so close. Nor that I was a topic of conversation between the two of you."

Phoenix was trying to get to her, but she wouldn't let him. "You know what your problem is?"

He blew out a breath. "I'm sure you'll tell me."

She smiled and went on. "Your problem is that you expect someone else to fix this for you." Her bluntness could wind up costing her career, but no one else was inclined to stand up to him. The sooner he was back on his feet, literally and figuratively, the sooner he would leave the resort and things would get back to normal.

Sierra ignored the twinge of regret the thought of his leaving caused. Instead, she continued on, intentionally discarding any effort to employ politeness. Phoenix needed to hear the unvarnished truth. "You may not be able to do the things you used to, but you can have a happy, fulfilling future."

He cocked his head to one side, eyebrows lifted. "Are you happy, Sierra?"

The question caught her off guard. The way he said it, the way he looked at her had feelings she'd nearly forgotten bubbling inside of her. She chose to ignore his question and took a breath. "We aren't talking about me. We're talking about you. If you want to spend the rest of your life being angry and defeated, then I hope that you'll find somewhere else to do it!"

His mouth flew open in disbelief. "Are you telling me to leave the resort? *My* resort? Because that is what it sounded like to me, Sierra."

"No, that's not what I'm saying. What I am trying to say is that no one wants to be with someone who is angry all of the time."

"You didn't seem all that adverse the other day on the deck." His tone was suggestive as his gaze skimmed down her body before returning to her pouty lips.

"Don't..."

"Don't what?" he challenged her, his tone retaining all of its redolence.

"Don't bring that up." She blinked, in an effort to regroup her thoughts.

Phoenix went on to say, "Seaside Haven is mine. So I'll stay here as long as I please."

"You're right," she agreed calmly, even though her pulse was still racing.

"And I'm sure that you can find another manager."

She loved her job at the resort. She would be distraught to leave here. And to leave Phoenix. She puzzled over her feelings and wondered if she should apologize. She moderated her tone and lowered the volume. "Phoenix, you have a lot to be grateful for. You walked away from a car accident that could've ended your life or left you confined to a wheelchair."

He closed his eyes momentarily, and she thought she may have gotten her point through to him but then he demanded, "Are you finished?"

"I...I guess I am." And Sierra sincerely thought her career was also.

"Good." He turned and pointed to the tray of food that sat untouched. "I'd like to eat on the deck tonight." He started for the door. Apparently, he expected her to carry the tray outside for him.

Sierra picked up the tray. The cheerful yellow flower in the vase mocked her mood. She might be his employee, but she wouldn't be his enabler. "You carry it," she called out after him.

He glared back at her. "I can't and you know it."

"So you know what that means?" She didn't wait for him to respond, but continued. "You need to put more effort in so that you can improve your situation."

"Do you think this is how I want to live?" His voice had turned soft, but she wasn't fooled by the muted tone. He was every bit as angry as he'd been earlier.

"I think..." was as far as she got before he cut her off.

"I hate this!" he shouted, throwing the cane down with such force that it snapped in two. One half flew into the bedroom while the other half flipped end over end before striking Sierra in the face. The jagged piece of wood pierced her flesh. She reached and clapped her hand over the opening.

The color drained from Phoenix's face as he watched in surprise.

"Oh, my God! Sierra, I never meant to do that." He reached for her but she batted his hand away.

More frustrated than anything, she turned and rushed down the hallway, passing a wide-eyed Adam as she sought the refuge of her office.

Chapter Seven

Phoenix was disgusted with himself. Of course he hadn't intended for the cane to snap and strike Sierra, but that was exactly what had happened. His anger had caused her injury and all she'd been trying to do was help him.

He rubbed a hand over his face as he slid down the wall to the floor. Never had he hated himself more. Sierra was right. He had a lot to be grateful for. And his mother had been right. He needed to take responsibility for his life and be the man his grandfather had believed Phoenix could be.

He thought he'd been doing that by coming to Seaside, determined to learn the ropes and eventually take over the day-to-day operations of the resort. But he hadn't come here to heal, he'd come here to hide.

He was still seated on the floor when Adam reached him several minutes later.

"Mr. Chamberlain? Are you all right?" The young man's eyes were wide with concern.

Phoenix wasn't sure how to respond. He wasn't all right, but it had nothing to do with his leg. So, instead of answering Adam's question, he asked, "Can you help me up from here?"

"Sure boss."

With Adam's assistance, Phoenix was soon on his feet.

"What happened to your cane?" Adam asked.

Phoenix's stomach clenched with a mixture of embarrassment and shame. "I'd rather not talk about that."

"Okay, no problem." The therapist bobbed his head in affirmation.

That was Adam, eager to please, but unable to criticize his boss for his lack of effort and bad attitude. Unlike Sierra, who'd called Phoenix on both of them even though it meant she may lose her job. Phoenix pictured her face again and a fresh wave of shame washed over him.

"I'd like to lie down," he announced.

"Right now?" Adam frowned.

"Therapy tomorrow I promise, but right now I have a lot to think about."

The following morning, Adam helped Phoenix out to the deck before the sun was fully up. He'd hoped to find Sierra there, drinking coffee, the bible open on her lap. God knew, he needed to beg for forgiveness. But the deck was empty.

"Looks like we beat Sierra out here today," he said in what he hoped was a conversation starter rather than an attempt to question her whereabouts.

Adam helped lower him into one of the lounge chairs before he replied, "She may be sleeping late today."

"Oh, why is that?" Phoenix asked.

"She didn't get back from the emergency room until after two this morning."

"Emergency room?" Phoenix swallowed hard. "How bad was the gash?"

"Pretty bad but they were able to close it with a few stitches." Adam studied Phoenix without blinking. Questions brewed in his mind but he didn't prod.

Phoenix didn't owe his employee an explanation, but he felt the need to clear the air. "It was my fault. I broke my cane and the halves went flying. One of them struck Sierra in the face." He swallowed again but he couldn't get the bad taste out of his mouth.

Adam glared at his boss. He'd never known the easy-going, carefree man to be violent. "So, it was an accident?" he asked, some of the tension subsiding from his brow.

Phoenix nodded. "Yes, of course, it was an accident. She was only trying to help me."

But it was time that he helped himself. That was the realization Phoenix had come to last night, as he'd replayed his conversation with Sierra and how he'd spent the past three months since the car accident. It had taken a beautiful, blunt-spoken woman to make him see the light.

* * * * *

Sierra changed the bandage on her face. In the two days since her visit to the emergency room, the area surrounding the gash had turned from varicolored red to purple to an unsightly blue. As for the wound itself, it was probably going to leave a scar. But it was her own fault. She'd pushed Phoenix to his breaking point.

For the past few days she'd done her best not only to avoid thinking about him, but to avoid him. She missed her early mornings on the deck, watching the sun disperse golden rays across the horizon. She missed Phoenix. But she took her coffee to her desk and kept the door closed as she worked.

As she replied to the last of the day's emails, a new one dropped into her inbox. She knew the sender well. The subject line read: Need assistance, please

Please? The use of manners was new as was his admitting to needing help. Curiosity got the better of her and she clicked to open the email.

Dear Miss Ramstad, it began. So they were back to courtesy titles. She should have been pleased. But disappointed was what she felt. She shrugged it off and continued reading.

Adam has the night off. Could you bring a dinner tray?

Thank you,

Phoenix

She closed the email and sighed. So much for her efforts to avoid him.

The room was quiet and dark when she entered holding the tray. "Hello?" she called.

"Over here."

His bed. Of course. The last thing she wanted was to confront the lion in his den, but she swallowed and walked over holding the tray aloft. She turned on a lamp at his bedside and set the tray on the nightstand.

Phoenix sat up and rested his back against the upholstered headboard. He wore a t-shirt with a designer logo embroidered on the chest. That was as far as she allowed her gaze to stray.

"Here you go, "she said in lieu of a greeting. "I think you'll enjoy it. Bijon's prime rib gets rave reviews from our guests." With that she turned to leave. She almost made it to the door before Phoenix said, "I think I will have dinner on the deck tonight."

With her back still to him, she grimaced. Then a forced smile curved on her lips as she turned and crossed the room to retrieve the tray. "Sure, Mr. Chamberlain," she said in her most compliant tone.

"I prefer that you call me Phoenix," he told her as he struggled to stand.

"I thought that since your email referred to me as Miss Ramstad…" She let her words trail off and shrugged her shoulders. For the first time since entering the room, she glanced at his face. The dark smudges under his eyes made it look like he'd gone a few rounds in a boxing ring. The growth on his face made it clear he hadn't shaved in days and his hair was unkempt.

His gaze was on the bandage on her face and an emotion she'd never seen before glazed his eyes. Where he had been ill-tempered and bitter at their last meeting, this time he appeared subdued. Her heart warmed in a way that alarmed her.

"Sierra." When he spoke, his voice was hoarse. "Adam told me you had to have stitches. Did the doctor say if it would scar?"

"Probably," she shrugged.

"I'm sorry." He bit off an oath, and reassured her, "I'll pay for you to see a plastic surgeon."

"That won't be necessary. It was an accident."

Angry and bitter, Phoenix had been easier to resist. But standing in front of her humbled and contrite caused her heart to skip a beat and that was before his eyes locked with hers. Under his current gaze she felt more self-conscious than she had when his gaze had first homed in on her bandage.

"Apology accepted," she mumbled before she hurried from the room.

She took his dinner outside, bypassing the lounge chairs and setting the tray on the wrought iron bistro table tucked into the corner of the deck. By the time she returned inside to assist him, he had reached the French doors. She held one side open for him and their bodies brushed as he stepped outside. He stopped and held her gaze.

"Will you stay with me?" Phoenix asked.

"I thought you'd want to be alone."

He took a seat on one of the heavy wrought iron chairs she'd pulled out for him. "I don't know what I want anymore. Except that I'd like for you to stay with me."

Her breath hitched as he stared at her. This was not the same entitled heir who had arrived at the resort mere weeks earlier. Nor was it the bitter man who'd neglected his therapy sessions despite desperately wanting to get stronger.

She slid on to the chair opposite his and adjusted the angle so that she could look out at the ocean. While he ate, she took in the scenery. She'd always loved the view and the privacy of the deck, which was confined on both sides by vine-covered trellises whose blooms scented the sea air.

It was a hot evening, the humidity almost oppressive. Most of the guests preferred the air conditioned dining room to eating alfresco. In truth, she was surprised Phoenix had wanted to come outdoors, but after holing up in his room for a few days, maybe he'd felt the need for fresh air regardless of the heat that accompanied it.

"Hot and humid tonight," he said, as if he could read her mind.

"Yes it is," she replied to make conversation.

Phoenix set his fork aside with a clatter. "You must think I'm the biggest jerk in the world."

Sierra blinked, caught off guard by his statement. "Actually, that title belongs to my ex-husband. Besides, it's not my place to judge you."

"Because I'm your boss?" he quipped.

She could have agreed and left it at that. Perhaps she should have.

"I did a lot of things I'm not proud of when I was…going through a tough time in my life."

"Are you talking about your divorce?"

It wasn't something she talked about often. Even with her sister or mother, Sierra had been stingy with the details. She'd found them too painful to recount, too humiliating to admit to. So she nodded in agreement.

"When it came down to it, I had a choice to make. I could accept things as they were, which was bad, or I could make a change. It sounds easy to do…" she sent him a wry smile, "unless you're the one taking the steps and not sure where you're going to land." She reached across the table and laid her hand over his. "Change is never easy, Phoenix."

He grunted. "I admire you, Sierra."

She blinked in surprise. She wasn't sure what to say.

"Did I render you speechless?" he asked after a long silence.

"More like flattered."

He shifted in his chair and grimaced.

"What did the doctor say about the pain?" she asked.

"It's to be expected." He muttered. "He offered to give me a prescription."

She bobbed her head. "And you turned him down," she guessed.

"Actually, I asked him for a non-narcotic alternative." He picked up his glass and took a sip. His grimace was comical. "I've been meaning to tell you, this tea is dreadful!"

"It's peach tea."

"Sierra, in the South, people drink sweet tea."

"Yes, well, not all of the guests who stay at the resort are from the South. As a matter of fact, they hail from all parts of the states. There should be some sweet tea in the kitchen. I can get you some, if you'd like."

She was already rising when he said, "I'd rather have a glass of wine." When she hesitated, he added, "I'm not driving. Nor am I taking medications that restrict alcohol consumption."

"All right."

As she started for the door, he called out, "Bring two glasses."

"Oh, no wine for me. I'm still on the clock." She winked. "Besides, what would my boss say if he found out I was drinking on the job?"

His gaze had been on the horizon, where the waves were white capping before they churned to shore. Now his eyes shifted to her. "He'd say have someone cover for you."

Suddenly she felt nervous. But she suspected the butterflies in her stomach had a far different origin. "One bottle of red wine and two glasses coming right up."

Chapter Eight

Sierra returned a few minutes later, holding an opened bottle of merlot in one hand and a pair of wine glasses in the other. Her movements were relaxed but sexy. Phoenix sighed, and sent her a genuine smile as he admired her approaching.

She poured the wine, set the bottle aside, and slipped into her seat.

"Thank you," he said.

"For?" Her eyebrows shot up.

"Everything." He sent her a sideways smile as he lifted his glass and tapped it against hers. After the toast, they both took a sip. Then he continued, "This is good, but you should have picked one of the pricier labels from the Rondé Winery."

"This vintage earned a couple of prestigious awards last year, which is why Bijon asked me to order some to serve here at the resort. According to him, it pairs well with the stuffed tenderloin."

Phoenix glanced her way and nodded. "Are you a connoisseur?" he asked.

She took another sip, and then replied, "I wouldn't say that."

"I'm sure you know more about wine than I do." He held up his glass as he studied the deep red wine in the waning light. "I've never been able to pick up on the aromas that the experts talk about."

She wrinkled her nose and settled back in her chair.

Phoenix was becoming relaxed. His shoulder muscles, which were always so tense, had started to loosen. And while his leg still ached, he was able to ignore it.

"Don't tell Bijon," she said.

"About the wine?" he quizzed, surprised by her request. "A glass of wine shouldn't hurt you."

Suddenly regretting that she had said anything, she added, "He has this holistic approach to diet and nutrition."

He nodded. "Wine is good for you. In moderation, of course. Besides, Jesus turned water into wine."

Her eyes held as much amusement as challenge when she replied, "Never heard you reference the Holy Bible before."

Phoenix grunted out an affirmation.

She sipped her wine. The sound of the waves and the squawk of seagulls hunting their evening meal occasionally broke the silence. As did snippets of conversation from beachcombers or guests on the resort's public decks.

"I love this place." He didn't realize he had spoken the words aloud until she glanced his way, so he went on. "I came here every summer when I was a child."

"Must have been fun," she murmured.

Phoenix shook his head, reminiscing the days spent here at the resort with his grandfather.

They sat in silence again as the sun began to set. Words weren't necessary with her and he liked that. Most of the women he knew would have become agitated, feeling ignored. Sierra merely sipped her wine, seeming to appreciate the view and the calming sound of the ocean as much as he did.

The resort's shadow crept steadily over the beach as the sun began its descent. Just less than half a bottle remained, and Sierra wanted to stay for another round. But before she could say it, he announced, "It's time to call it a night."

"I was thinking the same thing," she said reluctantly, rising to her feet. She touched his shoulder. "This was nice."

Was she referring to the wine? Or spending time with him? But he stopped himself from asking her.

She loaded up the dinner tray while he managed to stand. His muscles were stiff from sitting. He didn't bother trying to camouflage his discomfort. Sierra stepped closer and put one of her arms around his waist for support.

The heat from her fingers radiated through the nylon fabric of his shirt. But what grabbed his libido's attention was the way the side of her breasts pressed against his ribs.

Firm but soft at the same time, much like the woman herself. And her attitude appealed to him as much as the curve of her hips or her dark-lashed green eyes.

Phoenix burned with dormant desires. Did she feel it, too? He recalled the kiss they'd shared and his breath hitched.

"Are you okay?' she asked, staring up at him.

"Yeah, I'll be okay," he murmured. "I just need to lie down."

His ardor cooled substantially when he spotted Adam sitting on the sofa in his room. He glanced up from the movie he was watching. "Is everything okay, Mr. C?" he asked as he rose to his feet.

"I thought you and Tommy had gone out for the night." Phoenix said.

"The band wasn't very good so we decided to come back earlier than planned. Let me give you a hand." Adam started forward, but Sierra waved him off.

Phoenix grunted before admitting, "I'm paying the price for my disobedience. You've done your best to help me, Adam. But I haven't been a good patient. That changes tomorrow."

"So, boss, physical therapy at ten?" Adam quizzed, his expression showing pleasure.

"Sure!" Phoenix replied, his gaze shifting to Sierra. "I'm not going to give up!"

Chapter Nine

Sierra slipped from bed before the alarm went off the following morning. She hadn't slept well. Even though she'd dropped off to sleep not too long after her head hit the pillow, she'd awaken just after five. She blamed the wine but she knew it was thoughts of Phoenix that kept her awake.

He could be stubborn but he could also admit when he was wrong. Just when she'd been ready to write him off as shallow, he'd surprised her. The man wasn't as superficial as she'd assumed. Not only was she physically attracted to him, she'd actually begun to like him.

She thought of the glimpses into his life that he had allowed her the previous evening. Apparently, even before the accident, his life was far from perfect. God knew it was easier for her to think of him as pampered and spoiled which to her meant hard to please and hard to love.

Outside her room, Sierra could hear footsteps. She figured it was Adam, eager to start his day. Phoenix's resoluteness the night before had seemed sincere, but would he do his physical therapy today?

"Just a minute," she called when a light tap sounded at the door. She pulled on a robe and loosely tied it for modesty's sake. It wasn't Adam who stood at the doorway, but Phoenix. Some of his hair stuck up at the crown as if he'd just gotten out of bed. Still, her heart somersaulted at the sight of him.

"Morning." His voice was scruffy from sleep but his eyes were alert as he did a quick glance of her body.

Sierra's blood heated.

"Good morning. You're up early."

"I couldn't sleep," he said.

She eyed him for a moment, hoping it had been thoughts of her that had kept him awake. "Are you eager to get started with Adam?"

"Sure." Phoenix tucked his hands into the pockets of his black track pants. But what caught her attention was his University of Georgia t-shirt. She was wearing one just like it.

"Nice shirt," she declared.

He glanced down, then back up at her. "Thanks."

When she pulled the lapels of her robe open to show him her t-shirt, her taut nipples strained against the fabric beneath the UGA logo.

When his gaze lingered, her flesh prickled with desire. Sierra hadn't been with a man since her divorce. For that matter, she'd been on only a few dates, set up by her well-meaning mother.

And when it came to Phoenix she was playing with fire. He owned the resort and he was her boss. Even though this was her home and her career, it was her heart that was at stake. She swallowed and pushed the thought aside. She needed to be smart and level-headed. So she tugged the robes lapels together and folded her arms across her chest.

"Did you need something?" she asked, intending the question to be polite rather than provocative.

Given the desire that burned in his eyes, she had an idea in which direction his mind had veered. God help her she thought to herself as her mind wandered.

He glanced away, and then replied, "I wanted to let you know that I won't be having coffee on the deck this morning."

Disappointment washed over her.

When she didn't speak, Phoenix added, "I decided to get the torture session over first thing." A sheepish grin accompanied the words.

"Ah, I see," she quipped, keeping their chat friendly.

At that moment, Adam sauntered down the hallway. He was dressed in a t-shirt and the same style track pants as Phoenix. But unlike his boss, Adam's hair was damp from a shower. "Ready to get started?"

Phoenix grimaced, and then replied, "No pain, no gain!"

"That's right, Mr. C." Adam's gaze shifted to Sierra. "I thought we'd start with some stretching exercises and then move on to the strengthening ones. But eventually, we'll need to use the equipment in your room."

"Of course. That won't be a problem." She sent Phoenix an encouraging smile. "Good luck!"

Around noon that day, Phoenix made his way to the dining room. He was tired and sore from his therapy session, but he refused to lie down. Not only because he'd promised Adam but because Sierra had said she'd join him for lunch.

"Phoenix Chamberlain, is that you?" a familiar voice cried out.

He turned to find Monica Swarovski crossing the floor to his table. At one time the two of them had dated. Not surprisingly, Monica had wanted to get married. Phoenix, meanwhile, had wanted to defy death on the slopes. She had been a vivacious, black-haired beauty. Even so, he had no regrets.

When Monica reached his table, he tried to stand.

"Oh no, don't get up." She pressed her perfectly manicured hand to his shoulder and then leaned down to kiss his cheek. "I ran into your mother and father at the country club."

Before she could say anything else, he corrected her. "My stepfather."

"Anyway, she told me that you were here." Monica's tone turned sweet with empathy. "How are you dear?"

"I'm fine," he answered, offering a patronizing smile.

"I've been worried about you, Phoenix. If there's anything I can do for you, just ask." She leaned in closer, showing off her cleavage, and said barely above a whisper, "I never got over you."

Just as Monica made her confession, Sierra walked up to the table. With one brow arched, her gaze slid from Phoenix to the woman standing there. "Should I get another chair?" she asked.

Monica peered at her, noticing the resort's logo on her shirt, and replied, "The table already has two chairs."

"Yes, but they're both taken," Sierra stated as she dropped into the vacant chair.

Monica transferred her outraged glare from Sierra to Phoenix. Not sure what to say, he made introductions. "Sierra Ramstad, this is *Mrs.* Monica Swarovski," adding an emphasis on the Mrs. "Monica, Sierra."

"Sierra, I see that you work here." Monica's tone was condescending. "Phoenix and I dated and we're still very close," she added.

"That's nice," Sierra quipped, using the same mocking tone.

Monica's eyes narrowed. "Phoenix and I were having a private conversation. If you will excuse yourself."

"Shall I leave?" Sierra asked him.

"No, we had a lunch date." He shifted his gaze to Monica. "My days on the slopes are over, he stated," surprised by the absence of bitterness. "But there's really no need for your concern."

"Oh, Phoenix," Monica wailed, her tone dry.

"Shall I leave you two alone?" Sierra asked again.

"There's no need. Monica won't be staying." He returned his gaze back to the dark-haired raven.

She pursed her lips together and nodded. "If you need me, you know how to reach me." She shot Sierra a pointed look before leaning over to kiss Phoenix on the cheek. Then she turned to leave.

Sierra smiled. She seemed content, happy. To him, she was beautiful, and growing more so with each new day. For the first time in his life, Phoenix was falling in love.

The cane Sierra had ordered online for Phoenix had finally arrived. It was black with an ornately carved handle inlaid with mother-of-pearl. It had character, unlike the replacement Adam had purchased at a local drugstore.

"I have a surprise for you," she told him.

His gaze lingered on her mouth. "A surprise," he quipped with a grin.

"I just need to make a quick call," she said, ringing Adam from her cell. He answered immediately since he'd been expecting her call.

"Now." That was all Sierra said before hanging up.

"Very cryptic," Phoenix murmured. "You definitely have me intrigued."

He changed his tone as soon as Adam came in carrying the cane. "I wonder what it could be," he said dryly as he took the cane from Adam, who turned to walk away.

Phoenix glanced over at her then. "Thank you," he replied with feeling.

Chapter Ten

"Going for your walk?" Phoenix asked the following evening as Sierra laced up her shoes. She had changed into shorts and he took the opportunity to admire her toned legs.

"That's right. I won't be gone long."

Since their lunch the day before, Phoenix hadn't had a moment alone with her. Adam was always with them on the deck in the mornings and he was in the room with them now. Three had definitely become a crowd.

"Do you mind if I go with you?'

Sierra blinked in surprise. "For a walk on the beach?"

"Isn't that where you walk?" he asked slowly.

She looked over at Adam.

In exasperation, Phoenix asked, "Do I need to get his permission?"

"No, I just wanted to be sure that Adam thought it was a good idea."

"You had a pretty intense workout earlier. Are you sure you're up to it, boss?" asked his physical therapist.

The only thing Phoenix was sure of was that he wanted some time alone with Sierra. He smiled and nodded. "I'm sure."

Sierra walked close by his side as they made their way to the beach. Even though they walked on a well-worn path between the dunes, the progress was slow. Once they were on the beach, she pointed to where the surf crashed onto the shore. "It will be easier if we walk down there."

Once they reached the compacted, damp sand, walking was indeed much easier. Sierra skipped around to avoid the waves that lapped ashore in their path. Phoenix, however, had neither the agility nor the coordination to do so, which meant his feet and pants were soon wet. But he didn't care.

"You're doing well," she commented.

"Thanks. I'm trying not to embarrass myself in front you." He reached for her hand and stopped walking, forcing her to as well. He was tempted to kiss her but he had something to say.

"I know the kind of reputation I have."

Her lips quirked with humor. "So do I. I read the stories."

"And?" he prompted.

"Where there's smoke there's fire," she replied her tone wry.

A full-fledged blaze in his case, Phoenix thought. He'd lived carelessly, surrounded by people as adrift and unambitious as he was. "Let me guess," he began. "You believe I was a playboy, living off my trust fund, partying seven days a week."

As he spoke, the water frothed around their ankles before receding. Sierra didn't try to avoid it this time. He had her complete attention. He watched her closely and tried to gauge her reaction.

"Was I wrong?" she asked.

"No, not in the least." It was a hard thing to admit to her, yet the admission was liberating at the same time. "I'm not proud of it, but I was all of those things."

"Was?" she quizzed and squeezed his hand.

"I have changed, Sierra. I want to be sure that you know that."

She studied his face, wide green eyes unblinking.

His emotions were churning as forcefully as the surf. "I've never met anyone quite like you."

"Oh, really?"

His heart sank. It wasn't exactly what he'd hoped to hear. He lowered his head, his tone beseeching as he pressed, "I thought you felt...something for me."

"You're my boss, Phoenix."

"What if I wasn't?" he rationalized. So much was in flux, including his emotions. "Tell me you're not attracted to me."

She managed a strangled laugh. "That's not fair. You know that I'm attracted to you. I'm just not sure that I'm interested in a relationship."

Phoenix wasn't sure he was either. But he suspected her reasons were not quite as shallow as his. "Your ex-husband must have hurt you pretty bad."

"He did." The words came out so softly Phoenix was barely able to hear them.

"Do you want to talk about it?" he asked. Sierra's eyes widened with surprise. He chuckled drily. "I think I've become a better listener over the past few weeks."

The evolution of Phoenix Chamberlain continued, he marveled. And the woman beside him had played a huge role in his personal growth.

"I don't like to think about it, much less talk about it," she replied.

"Sure. I understand." He nodded as they started to walk again, their fingers still loosely woven together.

"Turner was a cop. A good friend of my sister's husband, Del. That's how we met. We had a whirlwind relationship…"

When she paused, Phoenix couldn't help but ask, "What happened?"

"You know I've asked myself that question a hundred times." Sierra frowned. "All I know is the solicitous man I dated and the one I married were like Dr. Jekyll and Mr. Hyde."

Phoenix gripped his cane with a little more force. "Did he hurt you?"

"Yes." It took her a moment to go on. In that time Phoenix's blood ran cold.

"Physically, mentally…emotionally," she admitted. Hand in hand they continued to walk and she went on with what he knew had to be a painful recitation of her past.

"The bruises faded so it was easier to get past the physical damage. But it has taken me longer to deal with the mental and emotional abuse."

Phoenix nodded but didn't say anything right away. They had both suffered devastating injuries, he realized, albeit in different ways. Hers had been inflicted on her psyche. His were physical and more obvious, but that didn't make them more debilitating.

"Sounds as if you could write a book," Phoenix said, trying to keep the conversation light even though he wanted to wrap his hands around her ex-husband's throat.

She sent him an amusing look. "I have entertained the thought."

Something occurred to Phoenix at that moment. "Does he know where you are?"

"I'm not in some kind of Witness Protection Program," she replied somewhat indignantly.

He sent her a smile, giving her time to continue if she wanted to.

She exhaled a deep breath. "That's my story. Are you sorry that you asked?"

"No." And he wasn't. "I am sorry that you had to go through all of that."

"Ready to turn around and head back to the resort?" she quizzed.

"Let's walk a little farther," he replied.

Phoenix was tired, but Sierra inspired him. Faced with adversity, she could have given up, but she hadn't. And he wasn't either. More than ever, he felt as if he something to prove to both of them.

Chapter Eleven

Phoenix certainly had undergone a transformation since his arrival in Seaside more than two months earlier. It was well into summer now, the heat outside almost intolerable even with the ocean's breeze. But he hadn't used that as an excuse to ease up on his rehabilitation efforts. Despite his grueling daily workouts with Adam, he walked on the beach with Sierra each evening.

Even more noticeable than his physical transformation were his emotional and spiritual ones. He appeared to have discovered a sense of purpose and seemed at peace with his situation. During the day, he could be found out and about in the resort, greeting guests or fraternizing with his employees.

And he'd won over Sierra; despite what she'd told him about not being in the market for a relationship. But what the future held for them was unclear.

Phoenix was getting stronger every day. That was the outcome she'd often prayed for when he'd first arrived because she was eager to see him leave. But now he seemed to be as connected to the resort as she was and she wondered if it was enough for him to stay?

She glanced up to find Phoenix standing in the doorway of her office. She hadn't heard his approach, partly because he no longer dragged his foot when he walked, but more so because she had been so preoccupied.

He was tanned from time spent outdoors and he wore a lopsided grin where the corners of his mouth used to be turned down with pain. Even though he hadn't had his hair cut since his arrival, he was ridiculously handsome. And the long hair gave him a bad boy vibe that Sierra couldn't resist.

"I'd like to take you out to dinner," he announced.

"Really?" she asked slowly.

"Yes. But this isn't business related, Sierra. So, I'll understand if you say no." He sobered.

Her heart did a somersault. She was nervous, although something had been brewing between them since that first kiss. But it had been easier to marginalize those feelings with the confinement of their professional relationship. Now he was making it clear that he wanted something more. As his employee, she urged herself to say no. But as a woman who found Phoenix attractive and intriguing, she wanted to say yes. And so she did.

Sierra had almost forgotten what it was like to get dressed up to go on a date. She'd decided on a simple black dress and conservative three inch heels. Both were a few years old and she could only hope that they were still in style. She put on a pair of insignificant diamond earrings and sprayed on her favorite perfume. Her sister called as Sierra studied her reflection in the mirror.

"I can't talk right now," she told Sienna almost immediately.

"It's Friday night. You should go out and kick up your heels once in a while."

Sierra hadn't told her family of her and Phoenix's relationship because she hadn't been sure where it was headed. Not to mention, Phoenix's picture was probably in the dictionary beside the word *womanizer*. Still, she valued her sister's opinion and let out the truth in a rush of words. "Phoenix and I are going out tonight."

"On a date?" Sienna quizzed.

Sierra took a deep breath and exhaled. "Yes, I am getting ready right now."

"Are you nervous?" her sister asked.

"A little," she replied as she examined her reflection. Her eyes were her best feature and she'd added more eye liner and mascara than usual. "Phoenix and I have been spending a lot of time together," she added.

"Enjoy yourself, sis. I'm just surprised, that's all. You haven't breathed a word of it to me," Sienna shot back.

"I'm sorry. I'm not sure what my feelings are, or his." She fussed with her hair, which she had put up for the occasion. "Whatever happens between Phoenix and me, I'm not going to romanticize it."

From the hallway, she heard the tap-tap of Phoenix's cane. Excitement bubbled up, breaking her outward calm. "I've got to go. We'll talk about this another time."

"Do you promise?" Sienna quizzed.

"Yes, I promise."

Then Sierra hung up the phone and opened the door. Despite all of her talk about not romanticizing her relationship with Phoenix, one look at his handsome face and she was lost.

Sierra stood in the doorway, a vision of beauty in a delicate black dress that hugged her curvaceous body. Phoenix's heart fluttered the same way it used to whenever he'd stood at the top of a ski slope gazing down. "You look amazing," he told her.

"Thank you." She smiled as she fussed with her hair. "You look great too."

He glanced down at the silk suit and tie he was wearing. "I forgot what it is like to wear something other than track pants and t-shirts."

"I wondered where you would wear all of the clothes that you brought with you," she admitted.

"I'm glad I did so I have something to wear for our date," he told her. She had accepted Phoenix despite his scars and disability or maybe because of them. She was an extraordinary woman and he wanted to impress her, to dazzle her. If that made him shallow, then so be it.

"We have reservations," he announced. He had made plans that included a sumptuous meal at Makati's steakhouse and a champagne toast to the beginning of what he hoped would be a long, happy relationship.

His plans were forgotten the moment their lips touched. Vaguely, he was aware of his cane falling to the floor, as his hands made their way to her waist and their mouths fused together. "Perhaps we should go now," she said softly, the words coming out between panting breaths.

"Yes, you're probably right." he admitted. His smile was every bit as cunning.

Tommy was sitting in the lobby when Phoenix and Sierra entered the room. He pushed to his feet. "Are you two ready to go?"

"Yes," Phoenix replied.

The driver nodded. "I'll bring the Cadillac around and we'll be on our way."

Although they were late for their reservations at Makati's, a hundred dollar bill handed to the maître d' apparently smoothed over any misunderstandings. The upscale restaurant was located in a newly renovated two story building. The first floor was open to all diners. The second where they were seated, was reserved for A-list guests.

As soon as they were seated at their table, a black-vested server arrived with a silver tray carrying two champagne flutes and a bottle of Dom Perignon. "Shall I pour?" he asked Phoenix.

"Yes, please," he replied.

Phoenix was accustomed to the royal treatment. She was dazzled by his lifestyle, but she realized it represented a world she knew little about; a world to which he would be returning in the not-so-distant future.

"Enjoy," the waiter said before turning to leave.

Once they were alone again, Phoenix raised his glass and said, "To you."

Sierra clanked the rim of her champagne flute against his. "To us."

Chapter Twelve

Only one week of the summer season remained. Once the Labor Day holiday passed, the town would be quieter and the resort a little slower until the snowbirds started arriving in October. Sierra was looking forward to taking some time off to spend it with Phoenix.

The past couple of weeks had been a blur of stolen moments during the day and walks on the beach in the evenings. The depth of her feelings surprised her. Falling in love with her boss hadn't been her intention, but that was what had happened. Even though he hadn't said so, she was certain Phoenix felt the same way. His touch and passionate kisses told her so.

It was seven o'clock, and Phoenix was already up and dressed. Just as she'd learned to be spontaneous, Sierra had learned to appreciate surprises. Yesterday, he had surprised her with bouquet of a dozen long-stemmed red roses. They were in a crystal vase on her desk, their fragrance perfuming the air.

And a few days earlier, he had invited his mother and stepfather to come to the resort for a visit. Sierra had assumed he wanted to begin restoring their relationship and she'd been proud of him for extending the invitation. Pride had morphed into shock when he'd introduced her to them as his girlfriend rather than as the resort's manager. She smiled at the memory.

"What's taking you so long?" she called out for Phoenix.

"Perfection takes time," he replied from down the hall.

"All I need is you!" she exclaimed as she threw her arms open wide, connecting with the vase of flowers. The vase of roses tumbled to the floor, spilling water over the hardwood. "Oh no!" she cried out.

Sierra opened one of the desk drawers, where she kept a box of tissues. A manila envelope, with her name printed on it, caught her attention. She hadn't put it there which could only mean that Phoenix had. But what was it? She reached for it and opened the flap. The roses were forgotten as she stared at the document she'd pulled from inside the envelope. She swallowed in disbelief and her heart broke as she read Phoenix's plan to dismiss her.

Minutes later, Phoenix filled the doorway and called, "Surprise!"

He held a tray laden with breakfast and two cups of coffee. As distraught as she was, it barely registered that he was standing without his cane. The only thing Sierra was focused on was the ache in her chest.

Indeed she was surprised. All this time she'd been worrying about where their burgeoning relationship was heading, it had never occurred to her that he might ask her to leave.

"When were you going to spring this surprise on me?" she asked coldly.

Phoenix blinked in confusion. His face reddened and a guilty grimace replaced his smile. "Where did you get that?" he asked.

"It was in the desk. I opened it because it was addressed to me."

"Sierra, it's not what it looks like." He limped into the room, sloshing coffee over the rim of the cups, and set the tray on her desk.

"You're a liar and a manipulator!" she yelled.

"Yes…I mean…no!" he stammered. "When I came back, my plans were to take over the resort once I had recuperated. I didn't think you'd want to stay, but I'd planned to give you a choice."

"How nice of you to give me options," she snarled.

"I know it looks bad, but I had this drawn up months ago. Before you and I…"

"What?" she asked flatly.

"Fell in love," he insisted.

But she wouldn't hear it. She couldn't believe what was happening. Her eyes blurred with tears as she studied the document. "You're very generous, by the way. I've been well compensated for my…*service*." Her stomach hurled on the last word. She felt used. And stupid, because she'd fallen in love with Phoenix and she should have known better.

Sierra fled from the office, not stopping when he called her name. She couldn't stay here now. She was at the lobby door, fingers curled around the doorknob when she heard a crash followed by an ensuing sob. She turned and walked back through the lobby and looked down the hallway. Phoenix was lying face down on the floor just outside of the office.

"Phoenix!" she cried out.

He raised his head. His face was damp. He was crying.

"Are you okay," she asked.

He pushed himself up so that he was in a sitting position with his back against the wall. "No, I'm not okay, Sierra!"

"I'll get Adam."

Before she could turn to leave, Phoenix grabbed her by the hand. "I don't need Adam. I need you."

She swallowed hard. He'd never told her that before. "You were going to let me go."

"Yes, but Sierra…" Phoenix closed his eyes and let his hand drop to his side. "I changed my mind."

"How could you forget something like this?" she demanded, shaking the envelope of papers in front of his face.

"You made me forget a lot of things," Phoenix stated. "You taught me to believe in myself. How to accept my life as it was and to embrace the future." He paused. "I love you."

I love you. The words snatched her breath away. She had been in love before. And her ex-husband had used the word but mangled its meaning. How could she trust Phoenix and love again? How different was this man from the brooding and broken man who'd first arrived and turned her life upside down with his edicts and demands.

"Do you really love me?" She whispered the words as she dropped down beside him on the floor.

"Yes, more and more with each day that passes," Phoenix replied, reaching for her. "I'm sorry. Please tell me that you'll stay here with me. I want Seaside Haven to be our home."

Sierra framed his face with her hands, kissing his damp cheek. Just before their mouths met, she whispered, "I love you, too."

Away from the Sun
Book 2 in the Seaside Series

*"For God so loved the world that he gave his one and only Son,
that whoever believes in him shall not perish but have eternal life.
For God did not send his Son into the world to condemn the world,
but to save the world through him." ~ John 3:16-17*

Prologue

Velvety red rose petals littered the aisle that was carved out in the sand on the beach in Seaside, Florida. The makeshift aisle led to a white gazebo laced with climbing roses and red satin ribbons. Family and friends, seated on either side of the aisle, kept their stare affixed her way.

Sierra's father, Andy Dalton, clothed in a snug fitting tuxedo took her hand and helped her down the steps. "I have never seen you look more beautiful." Her father's eyes glistened as he smiled down at her. "I am so happy for you, doll baby."

Emotion filling Sierra's throat, she squeezed her father's hand while her twin sister, Sienna, tried to arrange the train on her designer wedding dress.

The music intensified. Her father looped her arm through his and Sierra closed her eyes. Her father whispered near her ear, "Are you ready?"

Smiling, she opened her eyes and together they took the first measured step.

Sierra's gaze, through the fine net of her veil, tracked over to her mother, Isabel Dalton, sitting up front, her eyes glued on her daughter. Sierra's gaze then shifted to Grayson Faulk, Phoenix's step father, who was standing beside him as his best man. Both men looked handsome in their black tuxedos. And Phoenix's eyes were dancing with love.

When Sierra and her father had made their way down the aisle, and the music faded, she was standing before Phoenix with tears misting her eyes. He had never looked more handsome. More proud. Carefully he folded back her veil and the preacher raised his bible.

Once the vows and platinum rings were exchanged, Phoenix kissed his bride. Then he rested his forehead upon hers as he held her in his arms. "Thank you for bringing me back to life," he whispered as guests began to dance around them. "I love you."

Sierra's chest expanded to a breadth and width she hadn't felt before. A tear escaped and rolled down her rosy cheek. She held his hands and searched his eyes. "I love that every day I discover something new and wonderful about you that only makes me love you more." Their lips brushed again and again. Afterward, she rested her cheek on his chest and contemplated their future together. Dancing with Phoenix on their wedding day, Sierra knew exactly where she was supposed to be.

With Phoenix.

At Seaside Haven.

Chapter One

Phoenix Chamberlain wandered out from the hospital room, his senses locked in a mind-numbing daze. He had received the call at nine that morning and he'd immediately jumped in his plane and had flown to Martha's Vineyard with his heart in his throat the whole way. He and Monica Swarovski hadn't spoken in months. Now he had missed the chance to say goodbye.

Through stinging eyes he took in the busy corridor. The air smelled of antiseptic and death. A passing doctor, deep in conversation with the nurse by his side, brushed Phoenix's shoulder as he walked by.

Where was God's mercy? Monica had only been twenty five years old.

A woman in the crowded waiting room caught his eye, her ebony hair streaming over one side of a tight fitting red dress. She held a swaddled child in her arms.

Phoenix rubbed his eyes and refocused.

Beneath fluorescent lights, tears glistened on her long, dark lashes, and as she gazed back at him, Phoenix wondered if they had met before. When her mouth pressed into a smile, his gut tightened.

She must be one of Monica's friends.

The woman continued to pace, her slender manicured hand supporting the baby's head. Phoenix forced one laden foot in front of the other and, what seemed like an eternity later, stopped before her.

"You must be Phoenix?" she asked. Her flushed cheeks were tearstained and her eyes...

Her eyes were onyx in color.

Phoenix sucked in a breath. His gaze had settled on the lightly swaddled bundle when the woman in the red dress spoke again.

"Monica and I were best friends," she murmured in a throaty voice.

He inhaled, rushed a hand through his wavy black hair and tried to get his thoughts in order. "The doctor said it was suicide."

Monica had died of an overdose only minutes before he had arrived. He had touched her hand, still warm, and remembered the last time he saw her.

"She was found unconscious in the bathtub."

The woman's words caught Phoenix off guard. The back of his knees caved in and he sat down, suddenly wishing he hadn't. Taking a seat implied he wanted to talk. But after months of sobriety, what he wanted now was a stiff drink.

"She regained consciousness briefly and spoke to me before she passed away." The woman's lips were plump and the bottom trembled slightly. She repositioned the baby and lowered to sit beside him. "By the way, I am Sue Deveraux."

He swallowed hard against a dry throat. "You said she regained consciousness and spoke to you..."

Surely she hadn't spoken about him. Monica had been a wreck after their break up. On their last night together, when Phoenix had insisted that he didn't want to see her anymore she had been too dazed to speak.

The baby stirred and Phoenix took notice of his face, the shadow of tiny lashes on plump cheeks. He looked so healthy and full of life.

Clearing his mind and the thickness from his throat, he made his way to his feet. "We can talk more at the wake, Miss Deveraux."

"Please, call me Sue."

He drew his wallet from his back pocket and pulled out a business card. "You can reach me at this number if there's anything that you need."

Finding her footing, as well, she searched his brown eyes.

"I need to talk to you now, Phoenix." She stole a glance at the baby. When her gaze meshed with his again, her eyes were pleading.

She seemed sweet enough and understandably shaken, but whatever Monica had said, he was not about to justify himself to a stranger.

His gaze broke away and he waved the card in her direction. "I really should go."

"She told me that she loved you," she blurted out, jerking half a step closer. "She also said that she forgave you."

Bent over, placing his card on a nearby chair, he stopped, and willed away the lump in his throat. He wanted this day to be over. He wanted to get back home to Seaside Haven.

He straightened slowly and lifted up a firm chin. The baby was stirring, beginning to wince and cry. A part of Phoenix was drawn to the sound while another only wanted to stalk away.

Exhaling, he shoved the wallet back in his pocket. "There is nothing more you can do here. Why don't you go and take the baby home."

"That is what I'm trying to do."

When she purposely held his gaze, he shook his head then shrugged. "I'm sorry, but you've lost me."

She bit her bottom lip as if she were suddenly at a loss for words.

He studied her flawless olive complexion, her classic bone structure and the delicate curve of her jaw and despite the day, an instinctive flicker of arousal pricked his skin. What was it about this woman that seemed so familiar? Had he slept with her sometime in the past? He pulled back tense shoulders. No, he would have remembered those eccentric eyes.

"Look, Miss..."

"Sue."

He spared a tight smile. "Sue, I am not in the mood to play games. Whatever you have to say, I would appreciate it you would just spit it out."

She did not flinch or coil away from his candor. Rather her demeanor turned cold. "Monica made me promise her that I would tell you."

"Tell me what, Sue?"

"This baby is yours."

Several minutes of silence passed before her words sank in, slamming into him as surely as if he had been rammed by a freight train. He blinked rapidly, trying to catch his breath. He must have heard wrong.

"That's...not possible. She was married to Blythe Sutton."

"That was nothing more than a marriage of convenience. And you know it! Monica was pregnant and unwed and Blythe was hoping to get his hands on the Swarovski fortune." A tear rolled down her cheek while her dark eyes gleamed with quiet strength. "Monica's last wish was for you to take him, Phoenix. Take him home with you to Seaside Haven."

Chapter Two

Later in the hospital cafeteria, sitting across the table from Phoenix, Sue brought the coffee cup to her pouty lips, certain that she had never seen anyone look more drawn - or more handsome. With the shadow on his strong jaw — as well as his mood — growing darker by the minute, his spoon clinked as he stirred cream and sugar in his cup.

Over the intercom someone paged for a Dr. Grantham to go to ward two. And near the cashier, a nurse dropped her tray. The clattering echo bounced off the walls yet Phoenix Chamberlain seemed oblivious to it all. His intense gaze was focused on one person...His *son.*

From beneath her long lashes, Sue analyzed his handsome, Hollywood face — the cleft chin, the straight proud nose. How he managed to look both passionate and detached at the same time she couldn't guess. She sensed a fierce energy boiling beneath the mask. The man sitting at the table seemed to be made of stone. She might never know why he had excluded Monica from his life. If it weren't for little Preston, Sue would not *want* to know.

Phoenix placed his cup on the table, and then slid a blank expression toward the baby, who was once again asleep in the carriage, with a tiny fist bunched up near his face. Sue had been the one to suggest coffee, but after so long of a silence, she could not stand his chilling calm a moment more. She had a promise to keep and a finite amount of time in which to do it.

"Monica was a great mother," she told him before her gaze dropped to her cup as she grimaced under the weight of her guilt. "He is ten months old," she added, in case he was interested, but Phoenix only concentrated on stirring more sugar in his coffee.

Sue pushed her cup aside and glanced around the noisy room. This was never going to be easy, but could it have gone any worse? What was she supposed to do now? The man was as sensitive as cold steel.

"Why would Monica commit suicide?"

Sue jumped at his perplexed question. But the query was an obvious one, even if he wouldn't like the answer.

She lowered her voice. "Monica never got over you." His face hardened before he shoveled a hand through his already tousled hair. Flecks of gold ignited in the depths of his hostile brown eyes. Choking on raw emotion, Phoenix studied the baby, the line between his dark brows deepening.

"What is the baby's name?"

"His name is Preston Chamberlain...Swarovski. Monica refused to give him Blythe's last name."

Phoenix's gaze slid away.

Sue let out an audible sigh. Was this man a machine? Did he ever show any emotion? Hot tears pricked behind her eyes as rising emotion blocked her air flow. Nothing had mattered more in her life than the outcome of this meeting and if she had to brush an overindulged ego the wrong way to get results, then by God, that's precisely what she would do.

"He is your flesh and blood," she challenged. Her gaze fell to the sleeping child. "Would you want him to go to foster care?"

Phoenix's long, tanned fingers reached for a glass of water. "I do not recall saying that I wouldn't take him," he drawled.

"You hardly seemed moved by the idea." Sue slid back in her chair and one black brow arched.

"You would do better to not be so hostile," he warned.

While her heart pumped madly, his expression did not change. His dreamy eyes peered at her until a shiver rippled over her skin, heating her from the crown of her head to the tips of her toes. Not only was Phoenix dripping with bad-boy sex appeal, but he was as unpredictable as a caged animal. No matter how difficult it would be, she must keep her emotions in check, not only for the baby's sake, but for her own.

"This day has been hard for both of us," she admitted, "but I only have one objective in mind, and that is to make certain that Preston is cared for." She leaned in again, praying her concern would be there for him to see in her eyes. "Phoenix, he needs you."

A muscle in his cheek flexed. "So it seems."

All her life Sue had mingled with powerful men, including business associates from her father's law firm, investment bankers, and she had dated a multimillionaire for a while. But never had she met anyone who stirred such strong emotions within her as Phoenix did. His presence was so commanding, despite the day at hand, she could not help but be intrigued. Everything about him screamed confidence and superiority.

And this specimen of masculine perfection could not bring himself to even ask to hold the baby. Sue would not have been able to leave Preston with him and simply walk away, even if she had a choice. Her stomach churning, she kept her eyes on the soft rise and fall of the baby's chest. There was never going to be a right time to get the final request out in the open.

"There's something else I need to say," she murmured. "There is another promise that I made to Monica."

Phoenix consulted the time on his cellphone. "I'm listening."

"I promised Monica that I would not hand Preston over to you until you were ready."

While her heart hammered against her chest, the man seated across from her slowly and calculated folded his arms across his chest. "I'll admit that it will take some time to adjust to having a..." His words ran dry, but then he cleared his throat and put more depth in his voice. "The only thing you need to know is that I don't run away from my responsibilities. My son will not want for a thing."

It was not enough. Even if he had greeted Preston with open arms, she'd still need to keep her promise. Turning from the baby, Sue clasped her hands in her lap and met Phoenix's patronizing gaze square on. "I imagine you have plenty of room," she hastened to add, "and I am happy to pay for any expenses incurred."

The haunting coldness in his eyes turned to flickering questions. He cocked his head to one side and a lock of black curls fell over his suntanned brow while the corners of his mouth lifted in a parody of a smile. "Let me get this straight. You are inviting yourself to come with me to Seaside Haven?"

"I am not inviting myself. I am telling you that I made a promise to Monica to carry out her wishes."

"Well, it will not work." He shook his head, almost amused.

Sue drew back her shoulders. She would try a different tactic. "I know this baby's cries and his routine. And he knows me so it is in your best interest for me to come with you."

"I will have help." Phoenix said it without blinking and his heart skipped several beats when he remembered Sierra. How would he tell her that he had a son that he knew nothing of until today? Would she use her heart as her guide or would she be unresponsive and unforgiving?

"Miss Deveraux..." A glimmer of sarcasm rose in his voice when he amended, "Sue, are you sure this isn't more about you than it is your inability to let go?"

A dark emotion that Phoenix could not name rose up in her. "If I could be certain that Preston would be cared for and I could walk away with a clear conscious, nothing would please me more that to give you two my blessing."

His sarcasm faded. "Only I don't need your blessing, do I?"

Given that he was the baby's father, she conceded, "I suppose you don't. But then again, you don't appear to need...anything." She let the words spill out as she crossed her arms over her chest. She challenged his gaze, and then added, "Am I right?"

When he didn't answer, merely assessing her with those striking dark eyes, her core contracted. Before the heat consumed her, she doused the flame and rose to her feet. Walking out would not help matters, but she'd had all she could handle. Phoenix Chamberlain was powerfully attractive, but no way was he human. And before she left, Sue would tell him just that.

"I loved Monica like a sister," she managed to say over the lump in her throat. "But I don't know what she was thinking when she chose you to care for Preston." With unshed tears stinging her eyes, Sue steadied the carriage on her arm and headed for the exit.

Phoenix called her by name but she did not turn around.

One moment the cafeteria door was an arm's length away, the next Phoenix's impressive frame was blocking the doorway. "Where are you going?"

"What do you care?" She angled the carriage to swerve around him, but he shifted to block her path again.

"I care more than you know."

But she was done with words. She let out a jaded sigh and moved again. Narrowing his eyes, he moved with her. "So, just like that you are leaving?" he asked and she smiled coolly.

"Yes, if you would step aside, I'll be on my way."

"What about the baby?" he quizzed.

"We both know how you feel about caring for Preston."

A sarcastic grin tugged one corner of his mouth. "You think you have me figured out, don't you?"

"I wish I could say that I had the slightest interest, but I'm afraid I have as much curiosity about what makes you tick as you have shown toward your son today."

While she simmered inside, his gaze drilled hers for a tense moment before he loosened slightly. "What are you proposing?"

"I will relieve you of any obligation and take Preston home with me. And if you are worried that I will ask you for financial support, don't be," Sue replied.

The silence between them became deafening. Finally Phoenix asked, "How are you in small aircraft?"

Her mouth flew open then snapped shut again. Hadn't he heard a word she'd said?

"I flew over in a twin engine plane. There is room for passengers," he went on, "but some people get queasy on small planes." Though he had a feeling Sue was not the queasy type.

"I meant what I said..." she quipped, but then lowered her voice as a curious older couple wove around them.

"I want you to keep your promise and I want to give Preston a home. Come back with me to Seaside Haven."

A choking breath caught in her throat. Maybe Phoenix Chamberlain was human, after all.

Chapter Three

Sue clutched the passenger seat armrest as Phoenix's private aircraft touched down. He had given her one month to fulfil her promise to Monica. Four weeks, no more, to have Preston settled in his new home. She would have liked more time, or at least the possibility of an extension should she deem one necessary. But, in the short time she had known Phoenix, of one thing she was certain — he did not speak for the sake of hearing his own voice. He was prepared to tolerate her presence for precisely thirty days.

When she stepped out of the plane onto the floor of the hangar, the heat hit her like flames over an open fire. Today, like most summer days in Seaside, it rivaled a stint in a sauna. The urge to turn around and crawl inside the cool of the sumptuous cabin was overwhelming. Instead, she gritted her teeth and eased out into the blinding Florida sunshine.

"Welcome to Seaside," Phoenix jested.

Shading her brow, Sue cast a curious glance around in the direction of the raspy voice. Phoenix stood there, aviator sunglasses perched upon his perfect nose, carrying Preston in one arm and the diaper bag with the other. Smiling, she rested her hands on her hips. Nestled against Phoenix's chest, Preston looked content, which was a good sign that these two would be just fine.

Her job here was to do everything in her power to nurture an environment in which these two could connect and she would know that Preston was happy and cared for...that, God willing, he would be loved and appreciated. That meant she had to step back.

Watching the baby blink open his sleepy brown eyes and frown questioningly up into Phoenix's suntanned face and seeing him return the curious look struck a chord in Sue's heart.

There had been a shift in Phoenix's attitude toward his son. It seemed now that the funeral was behind him; he had begun to show a tentative interest in Preston. But this was the first time he had carried the baby, and while his walls were still up, hopefully these small steps were seeds that would grow into a mutually loving relationship. Maybe, despite her misgivings and the sinking feeling that had minced around in Sue's belly the whole uncommunicative flight here, her wish would come true.

Sue stepped forward but rather than reach for the baby, she cupped his soft warm crown and smiled. When Phoenix's uncertain gaze met hers, the urge to tip close and savor that hypnotic lure was nearly irresistible. His sex appeal went beyond powerful; it was mesmerizing.

Clearly Phoenix had not the slightest interest in her. But she could do without him looking at her like that — as if she intrigued him or as if he needed to know what her kiss might taste like. Those kinds of feelings were not only misplaced, they were dangerous.

When he arched a brow and managed to look both naïve and sexy, she could not contain a grin. "You know nothing about babies, do you?"

"I know they sleep and eat. Does that count?"

He headed off, his focus on the four story resort a short walk away. Sue's steps slowed as she took a moment to bask in the place that Phoenix called home. Seaside Haven was an impressive structure that radiated both sophistication and a proud sense of endurance. Sue envisioned lavish rooms littered with nautical decor and equipped with every modern convenience. She could imagine the menagerie of clients who had frequented its floors and the stories they could tell.

A flock of seagulls squawked overhead. Sue cast another resigned glance around the sunbaked landscape and then picked up her pace. Phoenix hoisted the baby higher on his hip and worked to force his leaden feet forward while Sue hurried to catch up. Fine grains of sand crunched between her toes and she cringed as sweat trickled down the center of her back. She needed a bath and a drink — a Martini with an extra shot of vodka.

Up ahead, the resort shimmered like an opulent desert mirage. Phoenix grunted and reached up to wipe his damp brow. For the first time since he had stepped off the plane, the finality of this situation truly hit him. He was deep in thought when they rounded the side of Seaside Haven.

A woman was coming down the side steps, wringing her hands as if she were nervous or agitated. Her gray hair was cropped short. Soft lids hung over inquisitive pale blue eyes. Negotiating the last step, the woman extended both her hand and a cheery grin. The woman's grip was firm but not challenging. "You must be Sue. I'm Jewel Waycaser, the new Events Coordinator here at Seaside Haven." In all of her days planning weddings and coordinating business conferences, she hadn't been a part of anything as controversial as what was about to take place here.

Sue nodded half-heartily.

"Phoenix has told me all about you and Preston," Jewel quipped. Not exactly the truth. He had provided minimal detail and only after some solid pressing. And even though Preston had been conceived before Sierra and Phoenix met, Jewel was not sure how she felt about him fathering a child with another woman.

Jewel moved closer to Phoenix and the baby. Her heart tightened as Preston peered up at her; eyes wide and alert, while he lay nestled in the crook of his father's arm. Soft, wrinkled hands went to Jewel's mouth as a hiccup of emotion escaped. "Oh my, isn't he the cutest little thing?" A tender smile glistened in her eyes. Her gaze darted to Sue. "I am sorry for the loss of your friend. I know this must be hard for you."

Sue turned to look at Phoenix. "It has been hard for the both of us."

Phoenix made a noise of affirmation, and the ghost of a smile lifted one corner of his mouth.

Changing the subject, Jewel asked, "Did the baby sleep the whole way?"

"Yes, he was an angel," Sue replied. "But I'm sure he needs a diaper change." As if on cue, Preston began to protest.

"I will take him," Sue offered, but Phoenix rotated the baby away from her eager hands.

Sue's brow wrinkled. "Do *you* want to change him? I mean, don't you need a lesson first?"

Phoenix sidled past the two women and up the steps. "I think I can handle this."

Sue was unsure that he could, but held her tongue. If Phoenix wanted to dive in to prove himself, who was she to argue?

Jewel couldn't help but notice that Sue's dark eyes were affixed on Phoenix's every move as they ascended the steps behind him. "You must be thirsty. How does a glass of peach tea sound?" she asked.

Despite the hot and humid temperature, Sue answered, matter of factly, "I would prefer a cup of hot tea if you have it."

Jewel let out a loud sigh as she padded into the resort after Sue. "You and Monica must have been very close," she quizzed, hoping to learn more about the woman that Phoenix had invited to stay at the resort.

Sue remembered how she had made it through the chapel service yesterday with Preston asleep in her arms and a run of tears slipping quietly down her cheeks. Whenever the raw ache of emotion had threatened to break free, she had concentrated on the pastor's calming words and the soft light filtering through the stained glass windows.

Phoenix had sat beside her in the front pew. Dressed in an impeccable black suit and tie, the set of his broad shoulders hadn't slipped once. Some of Monica's friends had recited poems and prayers, but Phoenix had remained seated, his brown eyes trained straight ahead.

Funneling down a breath, Sue nodded. "Monica was like a sister to me."

"Preston is lucky to have you."

Sue smiled. "Monica wanted Phoenix to care for him," she explained. "I promised her that I would help with the transition."

Jewel dropped her gaze. She had some reservations about Phoenix's suitability as a parent.

A loud shriek came from a nearby room and Jewel bolted from her chair and sped into a room to the right of the kitchen. Sue quickly followed behind her. Her gaze landed on Preston, lying bare bottomed on his back on the bed, which was set up against a side wall. Phoenix stood there beside the bed, his posture hunched, and hands out, gaping at a wet spot on his designer label shirt while the baby kicked his feet and cooed. When Phoenix had taken off the diaper, Preston had wet on him.

Sue cupped her mouth to suppress a laugh, and then she sauntered forward. "It looks like you had an accident."

"I wasn't the one who had the accident." Phoenix replied, as he touched the wet spot on his shirt, and then flicked his hand.

Jewel chuckled aloud. "I will leave you two to the task at hand," she said then turned to walk out of the room.

When Preston was cleaned up and in a fresh diaper, Sue picked him up and nuzzled her lips against his soft cheek.

"I am surprised he didn't cry when you yelled out like that," she said, rubbing the baby's back in a calming way. "I thought you might have...dropped...him."

When Sue pivoted around, her words slowed while her response system went into overdrive. Phoenix was grumbling, wrestling out of the soiled shirt. Sue unconsciously licked her lips as the breath left her lungs and a sizzling current swept through her body.

Phoenix Chamberlain's chest was sculpted better than any she had seen. His shoulders were broad, his biceps were defined and the expanse in between was dusted with the ideal amount of coal black hair. Sue's gaze dropped as if she were imaging what the lower half must look like.

Phoenix tugged the sleeves from his arms and dropped the damp shirt at his feet. When he glanced up from the floor, Sue was standing still, her mouth slightly open. Inhaling deeply, his muscles contracted as a coil of arousal snaked up his groin.

He acknowledged that Sue Deveraux was an attractive, intelligent woman. And she also had guts. When most people would have given in to Phoenix, she had stood her ground. She had insisted that she do right by her best friend. Frankly, he admired her for that. But this physical attraction was headed nowhere. He was married to Sierra. Even if he were free, this woman wasn't what he needed and vice versa.

The baby squealed and brought Phoenix back to his senses with a jolt. Shoving a hand through his tousled hair, he tried to clear the thoughts from his mind. When footsteps sounded down the hall, Phoenix swiped his shirt off the floor and wadded it up. Sue, seemingly needing a distraction, too, spun around toward the bed, busying herself with the baby.

Phoenix had mustered a cool disposition by the time Jewel appeared in the doorway and chimed, "The tea is ready." Her attention skated over to his state of undress and her lips tightened. "Can I get you a shirt, Phoenix?"

Phoenix drew up tall. He held up the wadded shirt and replied in a low, even tone. "I was on my way to get one."

Sue flicked him an anxious glance, then for something more to do; she performed a fidgety finger comb through her dark hair.

They were a man and a woman who had experienced a moment when natural attraction and physical impulse had temporarily taken over. It would not happen again. He hadn't brought Sue Deveraux here to seduce her. She was at his resort only for the baby's sake. He owed that to Monica. And in four weeks, Sue would be gone from Seaside Haven.

He headed for the door and did not stop to hear Jewel's reply to Sue's peculiar question.

"So do you think that Phoenix will be hiring a nanny?" she asked Jewel, conversationally.

"We won't need one," the elderly lady replied coolly.

Sierra had wanted to have a family with Phoenix. Now, ready or not, she had one.

Chapter Four

The pearl white Cadillac Escalade stopped a few feet from the side entrance. A woman leaped out and, without shutting the passenger's door, sailed up the steps.

Phoenix had heard the engine, rose to his feet and now came to a stop by the veranda rail. When the woman reached him, no words were exchanged. She merely bounced up on tiptoe, flung her arms around his neck, and her cheek to his, held on tightly. Then her mouth found his.

Sue leaned back into her chair, now obscure in the early evening shadows. This moment was obviously meant for two. Sue glared at the woman; slender and toned with a mane of golden blond hair, loose and lush. Her cat green eyes were filled with affection as she drew back and peered up into Phoenix's eyes. Sue could see how the woman in front of her might captivate and hold any man, even Phoenix Chamberlain.

With a fond but strained smile, Phoenix unfastened his wife's hold and her palms slid several inches down from his neck to his shirt. She toyed with a button as she gazed adoringly into his eyes and sighed.

"You're home!" Sierra exclaimed. Her smile faded as she added. "I wish you would have let me go to Martha's

Vineyard with you. I could have rescheduled the meeting with the buyer."

Phoenix found her hand on his chest and gently lowered it to her side. "Sierra, I brought somebody back with me."

Sierra slowly straightened. Then she honed in on Sue. Her olive complexion, high cheekbones and onyx eyes hinted at French descent. As their gazes locked, Sierra surreptitiously found and held the veranda rail at her back for support.

Sue's face flushed hot. She knew what this woman must be thinking. The accusation blazed in her eyes. But she and Phoenix had never been intimate. They weren't even friends, and from the venom building in this woman's eyes, the sooner she knew that the better.

Sue stood to her feet at the same time that Phoenix beckoned her over.

"This is Sue Deveraux," he said, then nodded to the woman. "This is my wife, Sierra Chamberlain."

An uneven smile broke across Sierra's face. "I don't believe we have met, have we?" Her eyes narrowed slightly.

Phoenix stepped in. "Sue is staying at Seaside Haven for a few weeks."

"Oh?" Sierra's practiced smile almost quivered. "Why is that?"

Before anyone could answer, Jewel appeared in the doorway, holding Preston. The woman's jovial expression changed when she recognized Sierra. "Oh, hello dear. I did not know that you were back from your trip."

Sierra was in no mood for small talk or pleasantries and she didn't acknowledge Jewel's greeting. Mindlessly her hand slipped off the rail when her startled gaze slid from the baby to Phoenix. Without knowing the situation, she assumed the child belonged to Sue and Phoenix, which caused her heart to ache. Yet she could not let herself believe the worst. She wanted to trust the man she so obviously loved.

Afraid she may leave, Phoenix grabbed Sierra's hand. Her voice cracked when she spoke, "Phoenix...what is going on...?"

"This is Monica's son and I am the father," he said in a somber tone. "Sue was Monica's best friend and she promised her that she would help the baby settle in here."

Drawing back, Sierra exhaled, and then touched her brow with an unsteady hand. *"Here?"* She quizzed then shook her head as if to dispel a thick fog, but her expression remained pained.

"Monica's son..." She breathed out again before her gaze pierced his. "And he is *your* son?"

Phoenix's thick brows pinched together. "We are not going to discuss this now."

"When are we going to discuss it?" Sierra retorted. "How long have you known about him?"

The line of his mouth remained firm. Turning, he set his hands on the rail and peered out over the picturesque horizon.

The anxiety in Sue's stomach balled tighter. Hearing that Phoenix was responsible for a baby had been a massive shock for Sierra and she wanted answers. Sue couldn't help but think that she deserved them. And yet Phoenix kept his shoulders set and gaze fixed on the ocean in the distance.

It was not her place to interfere, but if she could ease the tension a little by extending her hand in friendship, Sue decided she would. She edged closer.

Sierra's bewildered gaze whipped around as if she had forgotten they had company. Then a different emotion filtered over her face and she exhaled once more, this time with an apologetic smile. "I am sorry for being so rude. It's just..." She sought out Phoenix's gaze.

When he looked back at her, the familiar furrow between his brows was gone. Accommodating now, he reached for her hand. Sierra stole a quick glance between the baby and Phoenix before she looped her arm through his. With an elegant, slightly possessive air, she asked, "Will you walk me down to the SUV?"

Sue tacked up her slipping smile. If she had felt inadequate before, she certainly did so now. No wonder

Phoenix had married this woman. She was beautiful and ultimately gracious under pressure. What more could a man want?

As Phoenix pushed off the rail, Sue piped up, "It was nice meeting you."

Sierra's lips tightened even as they stretched into a smile. "Oh, it was nice to meet you, too."

After that awkward scene earlier, Phoenix had taken the Escalade out to the hangar to bring the rest of the bags in. Then he had mumbled something about taking off for a while. From the window of the lobby, Sierra had caught sight of the white SUV driving away.

While Bijon Invar, the resort's chef, had prepared dinner, Sue had enjoyed a quick bath. Then it was Preston's turn. He had squealed and splashed water in the bathtub until the front of her dress was soaked through. She did not want to dwell on the fact that someone else would be enjoying this time with him soon if she didn't do something to change that.

She neither saw nor heard Phoenix return, but when Bijon announced that dinner was ready, he appeared in the dining room. With his broad shoulders back, he had sauntered into the room just as Sue pulled her chair out.

The meal smelled divine, but Phoenix's masculine scent easily trumpeted it. He had just showered and shaved; his wet hair, slicked back off his brow, was just long enough to touch the back of his shirt collar.

When the baby was settled in the playpen near the table, Phoenix had threaded his hands, bowed his head and said a brief but touching grace. Sue had swallowed against the sudden lump in her throat.

As they ate dinner, Sierra told Sue of Seaside Haven's main dining room, with its grand crystal chandelier set in the center of a high, molded ceiling. That room was kept for guests. She and Phoenix usually ate in the small room off the kitchen. After promising to show Sue around the resort the next day, Sierra asked to hear all about Martha's Vineyard.

Phoenix didn't seem to care either way. He seemed more distracted than ever. While they ate dinner, the ladies chatted, watching over the baby, who played with his rattle.

When Preston began to grumble, Sue left to put him down for the night. She was disappointed that Phoenix didn't offer to help with the baby's first bedtime in his new home. But she suspected thoughts of Sierra and her reaction to his son weighed heavily on Phoenix's mind tonight.

Preston had drifted off without a protest. After laying a light blanket over him, Sue tiptoed back into the kitchen and found Bijon tidying up. He had suggested she join Phoenix and Sierra for a glass of wine out on the deck.

Sue had grown warm all over at the thought of being alone with Phoenix, which only proved that it was not a good idea. But she made her way outside anyway. She and Phoenix needed to be able to communicate, at least on some level. With nerves jittering in her stomach, she inched closer.

Stopping at his side, she joined him in taking in a view of the picturesque horizon.

"Have you ever seen a sunset like that? I sit out here admiring those colors, and know this is how God intended for us to live. Not chained to a computer twelve hours a day. This is paradise."

For once, Sue thought the same way. They stood there, saying nothing, simply looking at the rose-gold pallet.

"Where is Sierra?" she asked after a few minutes had passed.

"She had to go inside and make a phone call," he replied, his gaze returning to the sunset.

She raised her brows. "Oh, that's too bad," she said. A hint of a smile hooked her mouth and they fell into silence again.

Sue shut her eyes, tilted her face to the sky and let the subtle breeze whisper to her senses. She imagined the way Phoenix's hands might feel sliding over her warm skin; sensual and stimulating. Opening her eyes, she willed away those dangerous thoughts and focused on the ocean below. She wasn't here to indulge in fantasies; no matter how tempting, she was here to do a job.

Besides, Phoenix's affections were spoken for. Sierra had made her position on that very clear. Suddenly weary, Sue leaned against the rail. She shouldn't have come out here. She was about to say good night when Phoenix's deep voice drifted through the cool air. "Is the baby down for the night?"

Sue nodded, "Yes, he is down and shouldn't wake up till around six or so."

"I see."

When he began to walk, Sue threw a glance at the sliding glass door, then inwardly shrugged, and followed. "This property belonged to my grandfather," he was saying when she caught up with him. "I carved my initials here when I was a kid," he went on and swept one long tanned finger over an etching in the wood. He straightened and studied her. She held his gaze for several seconds, giving him a warm smile. Then he began walking again, a slow gait that invited her to join him.

"Are your parents still around?" he asked.

The snapshot in Sue's mind faded and she squared her shoulders. "My father is. I work for him at the firm, Deveraux & Donovan. My mother died when I was thirteen. She had cancer."

"Oh, I am so sorry." His step faltered. In the twilight, his gaze assessed her. "I bet your father is proud of you."

She nodded. "I guess so."

"You must be anxious to get back," Phoenix said, leaning against a weathered rail.

Her lips puckered. "I won't deny I miss the excitement, but…" her words trailed off. When she realized their gaze had lasted longer than it ought to, a blush rose in her cheeks and then heat spread to other parts of her body. Phoenix pushed off the railing and rubbed the back of his neck.

"How did you meet Monica?"

"A friend introduced us," she answered. "We met at a party and hit it off. She had the best laugh."

Looking off in the distance, he rubbed his temple. "Yeah, I will never forget her laugh."

On impulse, Sue reached to touch his arm, to offer some show of comfort. Instead, she said, "You must have missed that sound."

A muscle tightened in his jaw and he let out a long breath as he searched the sky.

Sue's expression sharpened then frowning, she angled her head toward the resort. "Was that the baby?"

Phoenix listened, and then shook his head. "I don't hear anything." His gaze caught hers and Sue's skin warmed. The way he was looking at her now, she could almost fool herself into believing that she, not Sierra, was the woman with whom he was married. When a different, more guarded look rose up in her eyes, he broke the gaze.

Sue chewed her lip. She shouldn't ask, but she could not keep the question down. "Does Sierra like children?"

"Yes, Sierra wants a family…"

Sierra hadn't shown any interest in Preston other than out of shock and suspicion yet she wanted children of her own. If she and Phoenix had children together, would she see Preston as an inconvenience? If that were the case, what sort of damaged self-image would being an unwanted stepson leave him with? Deep in thought, Phoenix let out a breath.

"It is getting late. We should probably go in."

He sauntered over to stand beside her as she checked the starry lightshow overhead. When she turned to look at him, his expression had softened with an emotion she hadn't seen in him before. She might have wondered what it would be like, having Phoenix Chamberlain's undivided smoldering attention focused only upon her. And yet now…As she stood there looking up into the shadowed perfection of his face, improbability faded into understanding.

How a bit of common sense survived the desire coursing through his body, Phoenix couldn't say. He did not want to listen to reason. And yet the danger…the dishonesty of this situation was as apparent as the aching desire. As much as he wanted to taste her kiss, he could not ignore the hurt this kind of scene would cause. Finding his strength and his breath, he turned his head away. His deep voice rumbled through the quiet night. "You should go inside."

Without saying a word, she wove around him toward the door.

Chapter Five

The next morning Sierra drove into Seaside, a charming town that consisted of a main street lined with palm trees, boutiques, restaurants and hotels which led to Seaside Haven.

Parked in front of Betty's Bakery, Sierra swung out of the driver's side of the Escalade and absorbed the town's aura of timelessness. She loved this place as much as she did the resort. It was a nice place to catch up with the locals who frequented the town square.

Sophisticated Sue Deveraux, on the other hand, fit in more with canapés and cocktails at five. She would probably find this place tacky and possibly unsettling. Sue did care about what happened to Monica's baby and Sierra respected her for that. But as soon as her job was done, she would be gone, back to the city and civilization.

Sierra had an uneasy feeling about Sue that she couldn't seem to shake off. After much thought, she had figured out what needed to be done and how she should handle it.

Now she strode up to Mrs. Betty, the friendly gray-haired lady behind the counter. They exchanged pleasantries, and then Sierra took her coffee and made her way over to a corner table.

Seated at the small table, the robust man, dressed in a blazer, denim shirt and pants looked as out of place as he felt. When Liam Nelson removed his black Stetson hat and stood to greet her, she squared her shoulders. Her blond hair was glossy as ever, but her eyes didn't hold their normal fervor. She lifted a large envelope and gave a jaded smile. "Sierra, good to see you," said Liam with a deep, slow drawl.

There was a moment's pause before a sigh came out. "Thank you for coming on such short notice." From her penurious tone, he sensed something was not right in her world. Then her green eyes softened and an inviting smile curved her lips. He pulled the chair out for her trying to keep his eyes from lingering on her attire: a short, silk wrap dress, the same color of green as her eyes. Positioning herself close, she murmured, "It is so good to see you."

His slim nostrils flared as he spoke. "So, tell me, how do you feel about raising Monica's son?"

She set her jaw. "That baby deserves a home. And there is no reason why we shouldn't care for him."

He rubbed his brow as he met her gaze. "How long has Phoenix known this woman, Sue…Deveraux? Struggling to pronounce her last name, he glanced over the notes he had written down the night before when he and Sierra spoke over the telephone.

She told him the truth. "I have not asked him that question. I met her for the first time yesterday."

"Then she must be manipulative, getting you to agree to her stay at Seaside Haven." His eyes narrowed. Sierra may have more reason than she knew to be concerned about Sue Deveraux.

Sierra implored him with her eyes. He reached across the table and found her hand, holding it between both of his. "I will let you know what I find out about her." Then he threw his black Stetson hat back on and left the bakery a few minutes later, reminding himself that the physical attraction he felt for Sierra was another matter.

Call me regarding the Lewinski case.

Biting her lower lip, Sue shifted her gaze from the cell phone to Preston lying, happy and playful, on a nearby blanket. Since coming to Seaside, she had noticed a decline in his naps. Rather than fight the change in what seemed like a set schedule, Sue spread a blanket out beneath the sprawling umbrella on the deck and for the past thirty minutes had watched him kick and coo.

While her father had been placid about her request for this unscheduled break, he would not have left that message without good reason. Sue set the phone against her chin as her stomach knotted. Had her father's disappointment turned to action? Had he replaced her on the case? She breathed in slowly, calmly. Her thumb was poised on the send button on her phone when she heard the sound of an engine. The same sound she had heard leaving the property early that morning. Sierra was home.

The SUV came to a stop and when the door opened, Sierra angled out, looking taller and more toned than Sue remembered. Everything about her spoke of confidence and competence. Sue pasted on a nondescript smile. When Sierra's gaze spotted her, she gave a quick wave and headed over. With each long, measured stride, her heart began to race.

When Sierra reached them on the deck, she glanced around, squinting against the sun sitting high in the cloudless sky. "It is a lovely day. Not too hot."

Sue raised a brow as Sierra squatted down beside the baby, her wrap dress opening to expose her tanned thigh. When Preston's rattle slipped from his grasp, she picked it up and shook it until the baby grabbed it and stuck it in his mouth.

A smile formed on Sierra's mouth. "Is he hungry?"

"He had lunch. What he needs is a nap."

The baby squealed and threw the rattle down again. Sierra chuckled softly. "He doesn't look like Phoenix," she said aloud, without intending to.

"Oh, he looks like Monica. He has the same cheeky grin." Sue countered.

Jewel called from the doorway. "Do you ladies want some lunch?"

Standing now, Sierra swiveled around on the toes of her shoes. "Sure, that sounds good."

Sue nodded in agreement.

"Can I put the baby down for a nap?" Jewel asked.

"Yes, indeed." Sue replied, then scooped the baby up and gave him a bounce before handing him over to Jewel.

Glowing, Jewel brought him close for a cuddle. Preston seemed content in her arms so Sue had no reason to cut in…except after Jewel and Preston's departure, she and Sierra would be alone.

As Jewel and the baby vanished back into the resort, Sierra gathered her composure. Once her gaze locked with Sue's, the message in her eyes said nothing about awkwardness or caution; she looked unnervingly assured. She offered a sentence or two, keeping communication friendly, but unquestionably matter-of-fact.

With a tense look, Sue glanced at her cell phone. With a finger swipe, she alleviated the screen of dust. Then, after a reasonably short amount of time passed, Sue followed Sierra inside. Distance and safety from possible humiliation accomplished.

Chapter Six

After lunch, Sue went to her room and sat on the edge of the bed. She had experienced a gamut of emotions the past week; sadness over Monica's death, protectiveness toward Preston, acute physical desire, and today, guilt.

Slipping off her sandals, she took in her surroundings. She didn't belong here. The walls of this resort contained history, and memories that Phoenix was a part of. And this cozy quiet room, with its nautical décor, off white furnishings, and hardwood floors, was not for her. Sue Deveraux was made for tailored suits and oversized classic jewelry, meetings and uncompromising decisions.

Exhaling, she studied her cell phone on the bedside table. She couldn't put that phone call off any longer. The secretary picked up after the second ring, with her usual greeting. "Good afternoon, Deveraux & Donovan. How may I direct your call?"

"Hi, Cyndi, it's me, Sue. Is my father in the office?"

"Yes, he is. Can you hold for a moment?"

"Sure." Sue gripped the phone in her slender hand as she waited for her father to pick up.

"This is Jack Deveraux."

"Hi…dad, how are you?"

He groaned a sigh of relief. "I would be doing better if you were here."

She fell back onto the soft bed. "Why, what is going on?"

"The Lewinski case has been moved to the end of next week."

Her eyes widened while her heart sank. "That is two weeks earlier than scheduled."

"They are eager to see what we have. I am eager to show them! What about you?"

She visualized her big mahogany desk in the corner office with a view.

"Sue, are you there?" her father asked after a moment of silence.

Her stomach knotted and she sat up. "If I get back mid-week, that will be plenty of time to do the final briefing."

Tension crackled down the line. "Honey, I understand that you were good friends with Monica, but you have a job to do…here."

Sue drew her legs up and hugged her knees. Her father was right. Given the circumstances, it was only logical that she get back to work. Still, she was hesitant. "Can you give me until Monday?" She imagined her father shaking his head.

"You have a job to do," he said, unkindly. "Either come back and handle this case or I will have to assign it to someone who can."

Her throat tightened. "But I have put so much work into that case."

"Sue, sweetheart, this is about business. You are either committed to this firm a hundred percent or you're not."

She let go of her knees and straightened. "I understand."

She really did. And yet leaving Preston here seemed heartless.

Her father sighed. "If you think you can pull it off, I will give you until Monday to get back."

She pushed to her feet. "Really?" she squealed.

"I expect you to be in my office on Monday morning, eight a.m. sharp," he decreed.

She agreed, said goodbye and thought about how her days at Seaside Haven had dwindled down, but at least she didn't have to hop on a plane back to Martha's Vineyard tomorrow. But now she needed to make the most of every minute she had with Preston – and Phoenix.

She crept the short distance to the crib and inched closer until her fingers curled over the sturdy rail. She smiled. Preston was still asleep. She stood there, studying his angelic form. In this moment of time, Martha's Vineyard and the law firm were another world away. And Sue was okay with that.

A creak came from behind. Heart pounding in her chest, she spun around. A shadow took on shape as it edged toward her. She smothered a breathless gasp. But as the figure walked closer, its build became unmistakable. It was Phoenix.

"Why didn't you say something?" she whispered, hoping the irritation showed in her voice.

"I didn't want to disturb you." He came closer and stopped beside her.

Bracing herself, Sue locked her weakened knees. She needed to stay focused. "I spoke with my father. He needs me back on Monday," she told him, frowning down at Preston.

His dark brows swooped together. "How do you feel about that?"

She tossed a reply around in her head. "I don't have a choice!" she snapped, causing the baby to stir. Gathering herself, she pressed her lips together and hushed her voice. "I only have a few days left."

"Yes," Phoenix agreed.

"But that doesn't mean that I can't come back."

The words hit him and he could only stare. "You would want to come back here?"

"I would like to come back…and see Preston. But only on one condition," she added to be clear.

He narrowed his eyes at her. "Is this going to be an offer that I can't refuse?"

She cocked her head and a lock of hair fell over her furrowed brow. "I hope so."

He held her captive with his dark eyes. They had known each other, such a short time, but she was convinced of his confidence and his pride. And he made her feel vulnerable, desirable; the way a woman should feel with a man. For so long she had wanted to feel as if she truly belonged, without fear of disapproval. Siphoning in a much needed breath, she sorted her thoughts.

Sue's gaze turned inward before falling to the baby. She thought of Monica – the promise that she made – and her throat closed off. She studied Preston for a long moment before her gaze found Phoenix's once more. His expression changed as he lifted her jaw. Sue thought he was going to kiss her, but he only smiled and murmured, "I make the deals around here."

Chapter Seven

The next day, back from her early morning walk on the beach, Sierra headed for the resort. She had agreed to go the gala charity event with Phoenix. In effect they both knew she had agreed to more than that. Knowing she would soon be alone with the man she had been physically attracted to from the start left her with an acute sense of anticipation that released a heat surging through her body. Striding up the steps, she chided herself.

Stopping by the kitchen, she expected to see Bijon by the stove or the sink, but the room, gleaming in the early morning light was empty. Further down the hall, Sue's door was closed. In passing, Sierra's pace slowed, but she moved on.

She came to a stop outside the partly closed bedroom door and peered inside. Life was known for irony, and a tragedy had given them a baby to care for. But Preston was more than Phoenix's legacy; he was the future of the Chamberlain bloodline. He would grow up, marry and have a family of his own. Perhaps settle here at Seaside Haven.

Sierra pushed open the door, a smile curving her lips.

"This is your great grandfather," Phoenix said to the baby, pointing to a portrait, which looked particularly regal in its gilded frame. "He was a clever man and very determined." Gathered in his father's arms, Preston stared at the stern looking gentleman in the photograph before Phoenix moved to the next one.

"And this," he said, stopping in front of the next portrait," is your grandfather, Phoenix Chamberlain, Jr." Looking at his late father, a familiar ache of loss rose in his chest. The finest artist on the east coast had been commissioned to paint this portrait, and the man had captured his father perfectly.

At the same time that Phoenix's throat thickened, Preston wiggled and he bypassed the other portraits until he reached the room that was his grandfather's library when he had been alive. Numerous shelves, laden with all kinds of reading material, towered toward the lofty ceiling. The leather chair and the cream colored sofa bore the subtle sheen of the finest quality upholstery.

This room upheld the Chamberlain promise of old money and impeccable taste, yet Sierra had managed to make the room look cozy, too, with fresh flowers, home décor magazines and crossword puzzles placed on the tables.

He strolled half the length of the room to the children's books and eyed the spines that he might read to Preston when he was older. The polished desk in the corner of the room drew his attention. He carried Preston over to the desk and slid open a drawer on the left hand side. The family album was still there.

Phoenix laid it out on the desk and flipped through the pages, pointing out relatives to a fist-sucking Preston. A bitter taste of emotion filled his throat and Phoenix swallowed hard. The pain in his chest intensified, but then, remarkably, the ache eased to a warm sensation. He had forgiven his father and released the hurt that he had carried for so long.

Later that day, Phoenix was back at work, but he was more interested in what was happening outside. Sue was pushing Preston in the swing that he had bought that morning. While pushing the baby in the swing, her face was a picture of happiness. Sue was attractive; perfect symmetry and graceful movements. He longed to join them in the shade of the umbrella on the deck. But simply looking from a distance reawakened a desire and he had to remind himself that his thoughts were out of line.

By the time Phoenix made his way onto the deck, a familiar engine groaned to a stop. It was Tommy Wynn, his friend and driver for more than a decade. Phoenix had told Tommy about Preston and Sue a few days ago. Guess he had gotten tired of waiting for an introduction.

Sue had scooped the baby out of the swing and Phoenix explained to her who their visitor was while Tommy was getting out of his vehicle. He offered his hand to Phoenix then announced in his gruff voice, "Seeing you have a guest at your resort, I thought I would come over and introduce myself. Tommy Wynn at your service ma'am," he said cordially.

Phoenix introduced Sue and Preston to Tommy. Tommy took the baby's tiny hand in his. Wrinkles formed at the corner of his eye when he winked at Phoenix and grinned. "He looks like Monica. Same grin."

His chest tight, Phoenix returned the smile. The emotion, he realized, was satisfaction.

Tommy eyeballed Phoenix, and then cleared his throat. "Where is Sierra?"

With a big smile, he dodged the question with a comment. "It might be time to take the baby in out of this heat."

"Yes, babies are sensitive to the sun," Sue reflected, dropping a glance at Preston.

As she moved toward the shade of the veranda, Tommy called out, "It was nice to meet you."

Sue shifted the baby and waved. "Say goodbye to Mr. Wynn, Preston."

When she had entered the resort, Tommy asked, "Are you having an affair?"

Phoenix turned to look at his friend. "Am I having an *affair*?" Affair wasn't the right word. Affair implied some ongoing relationship and neither of them was immature enough to think that was a possibility. They lived thousands of miles apart. Besides, he was married to Sierra, which reminded him, he didn't answer Tommy's question.

"Sierra had to go meet with a client, a man by the name of Liam Nelson, who is interested in purchasing a seasonal home here in Seaside. She should be back soon if you can stick around."

"I need to be on my way, but please give her my regards. And you can give me a call when you need me to drive Miss Deveraux to the airport."

"I will. Thank you, Tommy."

Chapter Eight

Sierra hadn't known what to expect. But when she and Phoenix entered the Gala Charity Ball, she was more than pleasantly surprised. Amid the soft strains of tasteful music, uniformed wait staff breezed around the room, decorated with fragrant floral arrangements. Best of all, their fellow guests alleviated any concerns she might have had about being overdressed.

Sierra's wardrobe had presented nothing even remotely suitable to wear to this event. She had a designer make her a gown and the pale blue ensemble made her feel like a goddess. The waist gathered high under her breasts, which created an elegant fall of fabric all the way down to her silver high heels. Her Bvlgari diamond earrings added the perfect touch and Phoenix was the perfect escort.

As he took her arm to guide her through the mingling black-tie crowd, she enjoyed a thrilling rush of pride. Phoenix's bearing was confident yet casually relaxed with every measured step. Movie producers searched for masculine looks as dramatically chiseled as his. Others in the room noticed, too. Women camouflaged their interest behind elevated champagne flutes. Men stepped aside to give him the right-of-way. Sierra had never felt more envied in her life.

And this gala ball was only the beginning of their evening. Phoenix had booked a room, at the hotel that was hosting the event, for the night – a night both Sierra and Phoenix anticipated. Every time he looked at her, she felt his gaze on her skin like a steamy caress. Every time he smiled at her, she wanted to surrender her lips up for his taking.

As far as Phoenix was concerned, making love was an art form, a living masterpiece to be crafted with liberal amounts of sultry skill. Sierra, on the other hand, wasn't entirely free of certain inhibitions.

Through a break in the chattering crowd, a waiter appeared carrying a silver tray. Phoenix selected two flutes and offered one over. Sierra took a sip, sighing at the crisp taste, and then she smiled. "Champagne is my weakness."

"Let's see…so is dark chocolate…and caviar…and…"

She laughed. Tonight the deep timbre of his voice alone was enough to leave her weak. "I like rainy nights, too, don't forget."

His gaze skimmed her mouth. "I haven't forgotten anything."

A man with steel gray hair thrust his hand out toward Phoenix. "Good to see you."

Phoenix shook his hand. "Hamilton Prescott, how are you? I don't think you have met my beautiful wife, Sierra."

Her smile widened. "Nice to meet you," she said cordially.

Phoenix and Hamilton went into a spiel about the sponsor of the charity event while Sierra sipped her champagne and enjoyed the lively atmosphere.

When Hamilton spotted another friend, he bowed off and Phoenix ushered her over to a long stretch of white clothed tables, upon which rested numerous items to be auctioned. "I love silent auctions."

Phoenix gave an obliging nod. "Then we will have to bid." His look said not to worry. "It's a tradition. And it is for a good cause."

The master of ceremonies called for guests to be seated. Sierra soaked up the conversation with their dinner companions, which included a criminal defense attorney and a friend who recently returned from a trip abroad.

Guests continued bidding until the lot was officially closed and the highest bidder announced. The room erupted with applause when Phoenix was awarded a painting by a well-respected artist. After dessert, the lights dimmed more and the music faded into a familiar dreamy tune.

Phoenix pushed out his chair and offered his hand. "May I have this dance?"

Arching a brow, Sierra accepted his hand. "But of course."

Once his hand was wrapped around hers, he rested them both against his lapel while his other hand lightly pressed on the small of her back. As he began to lead, she happily followed. The allure of his body as he held her close felt surreal. His step faltered imperceptibly before he continued to slow dance her around in a tight circle among other couples on the dance floor. "You look lovely in that gown," he murmured against her ear.

As her cheeks warmed, she offered thanks.

"I plan to hold you close all night." He murmured close to her ear. He was seducing her – here on the dance floor, amid hundreds of people. And the longer she drank him in, the more light-headed she became.

With a firm hold of her hand, he headed for a set of doors and didn't stop until they stood on a vacant balcony surrounded by a dark velvet sky littered with stars. He faced her and his palms sculpted over her shoulders, as he held her still with a mesmerizing gaze. His intense gaze lowered to her mouth. He slowly angled his head and his lips brushed hers.

Sierra couldn't quite catch her breath. Her heart was beating so madly against her chest that surely he must have heard the pounding. She had made the decision to come tonight. She couldn't go back and change the fact that her husband had a child by another woman yet she did not know if she had the courage and strength to go forward. But when he drew her close and his mouth slanted possessively over hers, she surrendered. Her acceptance and commitment was complete. There would be no turning back.

They arrived at their suite a few minutes later. During the short walk, Phoenix had held her hand while Sierra had chatted about how much she had enjoyed the evening.

He had never seen her look more incredible than she did right now in that sensuous flowing gown with her blond hair loosely swept up off her neck. He had been so taken by her beauty; he'd had trouble concentrating on the conversation at the dinner table.

Inside the suite, she moved to the center of the expansive room and turned to face him. He crossed the floor toward her, tugging his bow tie free. He pulled her into his arms, lowered his head and kissed her lips. Her eyes were closed, her breathing labored.

His mouth reluctantly left hers and he scooped her up into the cradle of his jacketed arms. Beyond a set of opened interior doors, the bed came in full view. The covers were turned down as he had instructed. With every muscle in his body tense, he delivered her to the bed.

He released his shirt's buttons and then reached to find the zipper at her back. His gaze fused with hers as he eased the zipper down. The gown fell over her curves and he soaked up the vision of her beauty. She reached up with both hands to release the pins and her hair cascaded over her bare shoulders.

He lowered his mouth to her throat and kissed her fast-beating pulse. She sighed and melted enough that she had to grip him around the neck to keep from falling back onto the bed. Listening to her heavy breathing, high on the scent of her perfume, he closed his eyes and trailed his kisses up her neck until his mouth found her moist, satin lips. He maneuvered her back onto the bed and as she wound her hands through his hair, he kissed her deeply, passionately.

Chapter Nine

Later, still floating from the effects of their lovemaking, Sierra lay with the sheet draped over her legs, drawing circles through the dark hair that dusted Phoenix's chest. With his arm around her and fingertips trailing up and down her side, she thought over the amazing time they had spent together. She had never felt more adored.

His chest hardened more as he craned to brush his lips over her crown.

In the shadows, she pushed up on one elbow. When she found his eyes, she sent him a mock chagrined look. "You are such a charmer."

"Do you doubt my sincerity? Because if you are…" he shifted until his face was an inch from hers…"I should show you how serious I am."

His kiss was tender and at the same time held more passion than any other. At that moment Phoenix wasn't her husband, or Preston's father. He was the man who had transformed her into the most desirable woman in the world.

When emotions pricked behind her eyes, Sierra broke from the kiss and wiggled out from beneath him. One minute she was floating, the next minute she wanted to cry.

She had experienced too much excitement and too many different emotions in a short amount of time. She needed to take a few deep breaths.

When her feet sank into the plush carpet, she dragged the sheet off of the bed along with her.

"Where are you going?" Phoenix cried out.

"I need to get some fresh air," she replied before she moved out onto the balcony where the sprinkling of town lights twinkled below.

Phoenix's hands raveled the soft and warm blanket around her and pressed in; his deep voice at her ear. "It can get chilly out here at night."

She smiled into the night. "I wonder what Preston is doing right now?"

Chuckling, he grazed his chin over her hair. "I imagine he is sleeping." He exhaled and his tone changed. "You are quite the mother hen, aren't you?"

A heart-warming glow filtered through her and she smiled. "He is such a sweet baby."

His smile grazed her temple and he loosened the blanket from around her. Sierra pivoted to face him. Her hand fanned over his bare bronzed shoulder. His eyes glistened in the shadows. His gaze was so intense; he didn't seem to be looking at her but rather through her.

Taking his hand, she turned so he held her again while they gazed out over the peaceful view. A falling star trailed through the star-studded sky.

"I was speaking with Jewel about the nursery," she began. "She told me that she would help me decorate it."

She had accepted that he wasn't going to reply when his deep voice rumbled over her head. "Sure…" He exhaled slowly before ending. "That will be fine."

Sierra was holding her stomach, her moist eyes shut. When she shivered, he pulled her closer and whispered in a deep sexy drawl, "Come back to bed."

After they moved inside, they made love again. Then they talked until dawn about everything from their college days and old friendships to their hopes and dreams.

Chapter Ten

When Phoenix and Sierra arrived at Seaside Haven the next morning, Sue was bleary eyed from lack of sleep. She felt saddened about leaving the next day. The time had gone too quickly.

As Sierra and Phoenix made their way up the steps, the warm sunshine on their backs, Sue was gripped by an overwhelming need to have this day stretch out before them.

Phoenix had offered to fly her back to Martha's Vineyard, but she had declined. Saying goodbye here would be tough enough. If he flew her home, she would be tempted to ask if she could fly back with him. The hopeless romantic in her wanted to be swept off her feet. But the responsible woman knew she had to return to her job at the firm.

The notion of spending more time here with Phoenix wrapped around her like a new promise and Sue's face flushed with hope and shame. The basis of her suggestion to return to Seaside had been to visit Preston. She had been so relieved when Phoenix had agreed. She dreaded not knowing when she would see the baby next.

They reached the top of the steps at the same time that Sue brought Preston out. She held the baby, his back to her front, so that he could see all the action. His little legs pumped with excitement when he saw Phoenix and Sierra.

Sue laughed. "He must have known you were coming. He just woke up."

Sierra's arms - but more so her heart - reached out taking Preston from Sue. She had missed him and now she realized how much. Sue stepped aside to let Tommy by with the bags. "How was the gala ball?" she asked.

Before Phoenix could answer, Sierra piped up, "It was wonderful!" The sparkle in her eyes confirmed what Sue had feared. Her abundance of enthusiasm at having spent the night alone with Phoenix had come across loud and clear.

When the time on her cell phone read four o'clock and she hadn't seen Phoenix since this morning, Sue was certain that he was either letting her have one-on-one time with Preston or he was avoiding her.

She had been in Preston's life from the moment he was born. She had rocked him and burped him long before coming here. She loved this little boy.

And what about Phoenix?

Closing her eyes, Sue sighed remembering his smile, his scent, the thrilling rush that flooded her body whenever she saw him. Had she fallen in love with this handsome man?

She opened her eyes and stared out her room's window. Preston was still down for a nap when Sue spotted Phoenix. A startling urge leapt up inside of her and she gripped the windowsill.

Fifteen minutes later, she was pacing the floor, waiting for the baby to wake. She was stir crazy; an unraveling ball of nerves. Over a man who hadn't chosen to spend these last few hours with her.

Clearly she needed to get back to her job and throw herself back into her work. Remember who she was and where she belonged.

She flicked a glance at the quiet crib and decided to walk out on the deck. She could hear Bijon's pots and pans rattling in the kitchen as she made her way to the door.

From the deck she could see the sinking sun painting luminous orange, red and mauve hues across the horizon. The night was fast approaching and soon the morning would be here. Her frayed patience snapped and she marched down the steps. Phoenix was standing nearby. His head turned and his gaze met hers.

Don't let him see that you are upset. She cleared her throat quietly; just enough to be sure her voice wouldn't crack when she spoke. Manufacturing a smile, she nodded her head in the direction of the resort. "Dinner is almost done."

"Great. I'm starved." With a smooth stride, he moved closer toward the steps.

When he continued to stand several paces away, his chiseled face so handsome, her heart contracted. She couldn't stand the tension a moment longer. They needed to talk, to sort things out. "Phoenix, I am confused."

His brows scrunched together while he shoveled a hand through his thick black hair. "Confused about what?" he quizzed her.

Sue heaved out a breath. The earth tilted. What was going on? Why was he suddenly so cold?

She moistened her lips and reminded him, "You said that I could come back here."

"You can come back any time you like," he said blandly. "It is up to you. You have your own life." He glanced at his Rolex watch. "And you should probably be packing so you can get back to it." He headed for the steps, but his pace slowed when she didn't follow.

She couldn't move. Her insides were roped into knots. If he thought he could walk away from her that easily, he was wrong. "I need you to answer me. Do *you* want me to come back?"

His eyes didn't meet hers as he growled over one shoulder, "Of course I would like you to come back."

"Phoenix, look at me."

His back expanded as he inhaled. He slowly turned and met her eyes. A muscle tightened in his darkly shadowed square jaw. "I am not sure what you want me to say."

She didn't give herself time to think. She walked straight over and cupped his face with her hands. Then, bouncing up on her toes, she kissed him. For an instant she felt a fire rip through her. She imagined she heard a rumble of satisfaction deep in his throat, felt the vibration rise in his chest and tingle across her lips.

But as suddenly as it appeared, the scalding tension faded away and the kiss…her mouth on his…lost its spark.

She let go of his face, found her footing and stepped back. But before she looked into his eyes, she willed all emotion from her face. The alternative was to break down and cry…

She eased out a breath. Shaking back her black hair, she pasted on an unaffected smile. "Oh, Phoenix," she began, "all I want is for you to know how much I care for you." When tears stung her eyes, she smiled again. She would not let him see her cry. She brushed past him before the tears overflowed and fell down her cheeks.

"Sue, wait."

She theatrically spun around.

They shared a gaze for a torturous moment and just when the emotion seemed about to break free – just when she thought she would crumble and tell him the truth – his shoulders relaxed. He sauntered toward her. "I'm sorry, but I can't give you more."

Chapter Eleven

In his lifetime, Phoenix had interacted with many women. But moments ago, the weight of the realization was like a stake being thrust into his heart. He was responsible, no one else, for Monica's death. And now he feared that Sue would have a similar meltdown. As harsh as he might have sounded, he meant what he had said.

Soon her time here would be reduced to a quaint story retold over Friday night cocktails with her friends. He would be the one left to care for Preston.

Forget about hurt feelings and meltdowns, Sue Deveraux was a strong woman. Even though she had admitted that her main motivation in her job was to prove herself to her father. She was strong enough to handle anything life dealt her.

But when an hour later, Sue hadn't emerged for dinner, Phoenix had asked Jewel to take a tray filled with the evening's meal to her room.

Phoenix hadn't been hungry either, but he ate anyway for Bijon's sake, then he took Preston out onto the veranda. He settled down on a chair with the baby on his lap. They were both keeping watch over another peaceful evening when Sue strode out on the deck. She tickled the baby's tummy, and then pulled up a chair.

Sierra and Jewel had also joined them and Sierra said, "We missed you at dinner."

"I sent word to Bijon that I wouldn't make it tonight. I had to pack my things."

Jewel caught on that Sierra didn't know that she had taken a tray to Sue's room and she smiled then sipped her glass of wine and concentrated on the horizon.

Rearranging Preston, Phoenix shifted in his chair. When he looked down, the baby was asleep. He eased up and headed inside to lay the baby in his crib, leaving the ladies on the veranda.

As he passed by the kitchen, it was empty. Bijon must have finished up and gone home for the night.

Phoenix entered the darkened room and laid Preston in his bed. Then he stood there gazing down at the baby. He reached in and brushed a curl from his forehead. He soaked up the vision of Preston sleeping peacefully and the knowledge that this was his son. After a few minutes, he said in a hushed tone, "Daddy loves you." Then he tiptoed to the door.

Chapter Twelve

When Sue's eyes dragged open, she wasn't sure of the time. Rubbing her eyes, she sharpened her gaze and honed in on the window. It was still dark, although it hinted of the coming dawn. She stretched and then winced when she crawled out of the warm bed.

There was nothing more for her to do here. Her mission had been to make sure that Preston was settled in and happy. And he was. As much as it tore her in two, it was time to return home. The message she received last night from her father confirmed it.

But there was a very good chance that she would see Preston again. When things settled between her and Phoenix, she would contact him and ask when she could come down for a visit.

Dressed in denims and a plain t-shirt, she had pulled her hair up in a high ponytail when she heard Preston in the next room. At least an hour before he usually woke. Did he sense something was off kilter this morning?

He was crying softly by the time she collected him in her arms. Rubbing his back, she crooned close to his ear, "Hey sweetie. Are you up already?"

Preston tried to smile, but he rubbed his eye with a tiny fist and grumbled again.

Phoenix appeared in the doorway. His alert gaze shot from the baby to her. "I was already up."

She smiled and a part of her knew that in the end everything would be all right. It had to be, for Preston's sake. She couldn't afford to be sullen or hostile. Preston's welfare was more important than anything else. Her insides clenched as she held him even tighter.

A few minutes from now, Tommy would be here to drive her to the airport. Sue nuzzled into the baby's soft hair and swallowed the lump in her throat.

Phoenix's deep voice broke into her thoughts. "Would you like some coffee?"

"I'd rather…" Her words choked off and she cleared her throat. "I'll get some at the airport."

He nodded. "I'll have Tommy come get your bags."

She inhaled a calming breath. A few more minutes and she would be gone from Seaside Haven. From Phoenix and from Preston. When he whimpered, she put a carefree note into her voice. "It's okay, baby." She pressed her lips to his brow. "Everything will be okay. I promise." She kissed his brow again.

Phoenix had headed off down the hall. Striding out, she followed behind him. When she entered the lobby, Jewel was speaking with a tall man dressed in denim and wearing a black Stetson hat. "I will let Sierra know that you are here to see her, Mr.…."

"Nelson," He added. "Thank you. She is expecting me."

After Jewel spoke with Sierra, she made her way over to where Sue was standing, holding the baby. When Preston saw Jewel he kicked his feet with enthusiasm. Chuckling, she scooped him into her arms. "He is certainly cheerful this morning."

Sue sighed, saddened to leave Preston behind.

Tommy and Phoenix came in after putting her bags in the Escalade. Standing an arm's length away, Sue turned to look at Phoenix. He turned at the same time and their eyes connected. She felt drawn to him as she had been so many times before. But now it was time to get back to other unsolved matters.

Sue managed to smile over the moisture filling her eyes. She cupped the baby's face and kissed his plump, rosy cheek. "Be a sweet baby for Sierra and Phoenix, okay?" Phoenix caught her last words, barely above a whisper. "I love you."

She didn't look back as she walked toward the opened door and slid inside the SUV. And then she was gone.

Phoenix wanted to take Preston from Jewel, comfort him, feel the connection that they shared, but he was not sure that was such a good idea right now. He blew out a shuddering breath, turned and strode out the door.

Chapter Thirteen

Sue's cell call connected at the same time the airport loudspeaker announced her flight was ready to board. She had checked in her luggage and grabbed a cup of coffee. Now she needed to do something that would lift a great weight off of her.

Her father's smooth voice filtered down the line. "Sue, sweetheart, your message said it was urgent. I meant to get back to you sooner." She could hear papers being shuffled. "I have been busy."

"Dad, I am resigning."

"I can get Kris Donovan to take over the Lewinski case if you need more time."

"I don't think you understand. I am resigning from the firm." She pressed her lips together as the silence at the other end stretched out.

Jack Deveraux's voice was deep and wary. "You are right, I do not understand! I knew that it was a bad idea for you to spend time with that man – and that, baby!" he snapped.

"Phoenix Chamberlain has nothing to do with my decision. And as the words left her mouth, she knew it was true. "Dad, you love what you do. I wanted to make you proud. I wanted to prove to you that I could be an asset to the law firm. But since I have been gone…" There was no easy way to say it. She sucked in a deep breath. "Being a defense attorney is not who I want to be."

"I see." His tone was calm, despite his temperament. "And what is it that you want to do?"

Her gaze wandered around the busy terminal as people arrived from exotic destinations and families departed in search of new adventures. She pulled back her shoulders and stood taller. "I want to move to Seaside. Perhaps travel and do some research."

When her father laughed, not in derision but a hearty, merry sound, she almost fainted.

"Sweetheart, I just wish you would have told me this before I spent all of that money for you to study law."

"I know, Dad. I am sorry." Sue shook her head. He had spent so much money, not to mention time and effort to show her the fine points of the business.

"Sweetheart, defense law can be cutthroat. At least it is here at Deveraux & Donovan. And that is not you. You are more like your mother."

The rest of his words faded. Sue had pivoted around. Now her attention was hooked on the terminal's automatic sliding doors - or rather, on who was striding through them. The air left her lungs in a whoosh.

"Phoenix?"

His purposeful gait came to a halt and he cast a hawkish glance around the crowded terminal. The look on his face said he was ready, and able, to tear the place apart if need be.

Sue swallowed to wet her dry throat. "Dad, I need to call you back." She didn't hear the reply. The phone dropped from her ear at the same time that Phoenix spotted her. He marched over with such determination, she wanted to duck and hide.

He stopped a few feet in front of her. Then she noticed that he was not alone. Sierra and a tall, robust man stood nearby. She recognized him as the same man that had come to see Sierra that morning.

"Phoenix, what are you doing here?" Sue asked her voice shaky and her heart pounding in her chest. "What is going on? Is something wrong with Preston?"

A hot hand clamped onto her wrist. She tried to wiggle free, but Phoenix's hold remained firm. Every muscle in his body felt wound tight enough to snap. "You told me that I was the father of that baby! And at first, I doubted that it was possible – the timing – didn't seem right. But the more time I spent with Preston, the more I began to care for him, as if he was my son. And that has not changed."

When Sue grew dizzy, she reminded herself to breathe. She lifted sympathetic eyes to his but Phoenix only tightened the grip of his hand around her wrist. At first he seemed to think her confusion was an act. Now looking into her eyes, she seemed dazed.

Sierra came close and her warm breath murmured. "Sue we know the truth. We want to help you."

The robust man stepped up and removed his hat. "Miss Deveraux, my name is Liam Nelson. I am a private investigator hired to investigate your friend, Monica's death. In doing so, I discovered that Phoenix is not the father of Preston. But more importantly, Monica is not the mother of this child. Which leads me to believe that you are the mother, Miss Deveraux."

Tears fell from the corners of Sue's eyes as her gaze shifted to Sierra. Sue detected signs of true concern there in her eyes and the terror receded just a bit.

Sue's cheeks were hot and wet with tears. Her voice was a desperate, elated whisper needing to be heard. "I have made mistakes in the past. No doubt I will make more in the future." Her jaw hinged. "But I did what I had to do…" Her words trailed off, and then she continued, "What my father made me do." Sierra nodded as she listened to Sue's heartbreaking confession.

Phoenix loosened his grip and let his hand fall to his side. She held her sinking stomach and pivoted to face him. "Phoenix, I am so sorry. I just wanted what was best for Preston. That is all that I have ever wanted. Monica agreed to take him at birth and she loved him, too. Then when she…" she let out a loud sob and let her head sag in shame. "I didn't know what else to do."

"Sue, you have been through so much. You need counseling. Please, let us help you," Phoenix pleaded. "We will see to it that you receive the best care that money can buy."

Sierra chimed in, "And Phoenix and I will adopt Preston. We love him as if he were our own. I have already talked with your father and had the paperwork drawn up. All you have to do is sign the papers giving us custody. And you can visit when you are doing better."

Sue had heard what she said, but how was she supposed to respond? Especially now when every fiber that made up her mind and body ached with such bone-deep hurt. The decision was up to her, but maybe it would be better for everyone – including Preston – if she left and never came back to Seaside Haven.

Remember Me

Book 3 in the Seaside Series

Continue to remember those in prison as if you were together with them in prison, and those who are mistreated as if you yourselves were suffering. ~ Hebrews 13:3

Prologue

Elizabeth Ben-David had never felt so cold as she followed the nurse along the dimly lit corridors of Martha's Vineyard Hospital. Their movements echoed like heartbeats along the barren walls. First the squeak of the nurse's rubber-soled shoes, then the tap, tap of her high heels.

When Elizabeth looked down, she saw the bright pink polish on her toenails. She had painted both hers and her daughter's just this morning. Julia had been as cheerful and warm as July sunshine. Now hours later, it was if the sun had gone down for the last time.

"You have ten minutes." The nurse's voice startled her, although she spoke in a hushed tone barely above a whisper. "The equipment can look frightening at first. Your husband is unconscious, so don't be alarmed. Hold his hand and talk to him. He will hear you."

"How can this be?" Elizabeth cried out. A faint hope flickered, and then died as if it were a flame in a harsh wind.

"The hearing is the last of the senses to fail," the nurse explained. "Besides, I believe our hearts are always listening. His heart will respond to you." She led the way into the small, isolated room.

Elizabeth trembled at the sight of the motionless stranger lying on the hospital bed. Her heart ached for her husband. Her knees buckled and she fell to the floor, kneeling beside his hospital bed. She stared at the bags of fluids that hung like Japanese lanterns around his bedside. The whir of a ventilator and the beeping monitor, that represented his heartbeat, were the only sounds.

He hardly resembled the man she had married. His wavy black hair had been shaved to his scalp, marred by a zigzagged suture line and bandages. His face was swollen with a stitched gash on his cheekbone and a bruising black eye. He looked as if he were already gone, despite the slow rise and fall of his chest.

Elizabeth held Nic's cool hand in hers. It didn't feel like his big, strong hand that she was used to holding. Now it was weak and still. *Lord, please, don't take him from me.* It was a plea from her very soul. She leaned her forehead against the palm of his hand. "Don't leave me, Nic," she pleaded.

The things that had occupied her thoughts earlier in the day no longer mattered. The only thing that mattered to her now was the life of her husband.

Please, Lord, don't take him, she prayed aloud, but she heard no answer above the noise of the machines. So she held on tight to his hand as if she had the strength to hold his soul to his body. Fear shattered her and she choked on grief. Then she felt arms wrap around her to comfort her, but she saw no one in the translucent light.

Chapter One

Elizabeth Ben-David slowed the black Range Rover and turned into the driveway of their home, a former bed and breakfast in the heart of picturesque Edgartown, Massachusetts. A town and house they had fallen in love with together. As she eased her foot onto the brake pedal, she turned her attention to her husband, Nic, seated in the front passenger seat. Since his near fatal head injury and coma, she was a stranger to him. She wished she could control the rapid beat of her heart as she watched him study the historic Georgian house in front of them.

Dear God, please let him remember our home. She knew it was a lot to ask, but she believed in the power of prayer. From the moment he had woken from a coma and through an extended stay in intensive care at Martha's Vineyard Hospital, Nic hadn't had any recollection of their lives together. All of the memories that they had made together were lost to him.

She did not know how it could be that she was a stranger to the man she loved so fiercely. Not only was he the father to their young daughter, but he was also Elizabeth's best friend. She had hoped that the sight of their home would spark something for him, but no recognition flashed in his eyes as he turned to look at her. "Who lives here?"

"We do." The words scratched like sandpaper against the back of her throat. She tried to fight back the tears that filled her eyes. "We moved in not long before Julia was born."

"Julia?" A frown formed on the corners of Nic's mouth as he repeated the name.

"Julia is our daughter, remember? I have told you all about her. She was named after my mother, Julia Grace."

"Yes, that is right." He released a deep breath and rubbed his forehead. "Is she here now?"

"No, she is at our neighbor's house. Mrs. Vie was kind enough to watch her so that you could take things one step at a time."

Nic looked truly distressed as his forehead furrowed in thought. "What is wrong with me? I can't even remember my own daughter!"

"Don't worry, it will all come together."

He gave her a lopsided smile which was all he had to offer.

She shut off the engine and reached for her designer purse without much thought. She had been praying for this day to come for so long, but now that it was finally here it seemed surreal. Disappointment sifted through her. She didn't realize she was holding her breath until she felt her lungs ache. She slowly exhaled hoping that Nic wouldn't notice.

"Well, we are here!" she exclaimed with dismal hope. When he turned his questioning gaze to her, she knew that he did not remember the place. It was a spacious four bedroom house with a sitting room, state-of-the-art kitchen, and a small sunroom off the kitchen. "Maybe once you are in the house, the place will seem more familiar to you."

He stared back at her with concern on his face. "What if it doesn't?" he grimaced.

"It does not matter, Nic." She replied, wanting to believe her declaration as much as he did.

As she stepped out of the Range Rover and closed the door behind her, she realized he was still sitting in the passenger seat, with sadness in his eyes. She wondered how he must feel to come home to a place he could not remember. And to bear the pressures of his wife's unfulfilled expectations.

She took another deep breath and walked around to open the passenger door. This was hard for her, but it was even harder for him. But at least he was here. She was grateful for that. She reached for his hand and as he clasped her hand in his, all of the love in her heart overflowed into her very being, giving her strength to carry on.

She tucked the keys inside of her purse and then tugged it up on her shoulder. "You can lean on me for support if you need to."

"I may not be able to remember things, but I can walk!" he quipped.

Her heart ached as she watched her once-strong husband struggle between steps. She unlocked the front door and held it open for him while he made his way up the doorsteps. She touched her hand to his and forced a smile. "You made it. Welcome home!" Then she dropped her purse and keys on the table in the foyer.

Nic was quiet for a moment as he gazed around the quaint room. He hardly noticed the rich colors and textures of the living room as he focused on the family portraits placed on varying tables and shelves. "Is that Julia?"

"Yes, that is our daughter." Elizabeth studied the professional photographs taken just a few weeks before Nic suffered his injuries. She turned to look at him and he had the usual lopsided smile on his face. She wished she knew what he was thinking and feeling. Determined to keep the mood uplifted, she placed her hand on his broad shoulder. "There are some pictures of you and me in the hallway."

"I would like to see them," he replied.

She nodded once in agreement. "Sure, but first let's get you sitting down."

He slowly made his way across the luxurious carpeted floor. She supported his arm as he dropped onto the posh, burgundy colored sofa.

"I'll be right back," she announced then smiled at him.

It frustrated her that the emotional connection that had always been between them no longer existed. Why had she thought things would be different once they were home? She knew it wasn't fair to pressure him and that she needed to give him time, no matter how hard that would be.

He had asked her for photographs, so that's where they would start. She grabbed a few photos from the hallway and made her way back into the living room. She noticed he was watching her as she came toward him. She wondered if he was still attracted to her or if she was a disappointment to him. She'd been spending so little time on her appearance in recent weeks, not to mention the weight she had gained during the pregnancy - and had been unable to lose. Suddenly she became aware of the faded, worn jeans and old tennis shoes she'd put on that morning and thought she must look hideous.

She slid the photos onto the mahogany coffee table that separated them. "These photographs were taken on our last vacation."

He stretched out his arm and snagged one of the bronze colored frames from the table. "Where did we go?"

She watched him carefully, but his face was unreadable to her. This was worse than a blind date with a stranger she thought as she recalled how comfortable she had felt with Nic on their first date as if it was meant to be. But this, now with him, was painful in so many ways.

"Try to guess where we were." She spun on her heel and retreated to the safety of the kitchen.

He must have noticed the family photo album nestled on the coffee table. As she put on a pot of coffee, she could hear the creak of the leather album's binding as he turned the pages.

Before Nic's accident, she'd worked part-time as a photographer. She had spent hours on that photo album. It had been the last project she finished before he had been injured in the hockey rink during a championship game. She didn't dare to think about her other client's photos that still had to be edited.

After pouring herself a cup of coffee, she peered around the kitchen corner just enough to see him on the sofa. Nic looked different from the man he had been; his big physical frame no longer as strong or imposing. Yet there were some things that had remained the same like the dimples that appeared when he gave her that lopsided smile and the dark brown color of his eyes. His face was lined with concentration as he studied the pages.

Emotion welled in her eyes. Stricken, she pulled back into the kitchen, longing for the pieces of their lives to be put back in place.

By the time she had loaded everything on a small sterling silver tray and carried it into the living room, Nic had leaned back onto the sofa and had the photo album open on his knees.

He looked up with a smile on his face. "That coffee sure smells good."

"Yes, it does." She slid the tray onto the coffee table and then handed him a cup.

He paused before he took a sip as she eased down beside him on the sofa.

He took a sip. "It is good!" There was that smile of his. How good it was to see.

"I am glad that you like it." She reached for her cup and then relaxed against the cushions. "What do you think of the pictures?

He took another sip of coffee before speaking. "I must be a lucky man."

She leaned closer to get a better look at the page. With Julia on her hip, her stomach was protruding. She frowned at the sight. Otherwise, the photograph looked great. Julia had been so happy that morning and her smile was radiant, just like Nic's.

"Julia looks so happy." Nic swallowed, as if he was struggling with emotions.

Somehow reminiscing how he had tickled Julia, so she was smiling when the timer on the camera went off, made her heart warm and made the distance between her and this different Nic seem less cumbersome. Maybe he would remember that in time, she hoped.

When Nic turned to the facing page, his lopsided smile widened. Happiness lit his eyes. He tapped the photograph where he was holding Julia, so small in his big capable hand. Another photo showed her little face staring trustingly up to her father's face. Nic swallowed visibly. "I don't want to disappoint you." Lines of frustration formed on his handsome face as he shook his head.

She laid her slender hand on his and realized he wasn't wearing his wedding ring. They had taken it off at the hospital. She made a mental note to look for it in her purse and give it back to him. "Don't worry about disappointing me, Nic. I am just glad to have you home."

He shrugged helplessly, unable to say what was in his heart.

"Your memory – everything – it will get easier," Elizabeth tried to reassure him.

Relief passed across his face and he nodded. His gaze fixed firmly on her as he studied the slope of her nose, her wide-set blue eyes with long, dark lashes, the contour of her cheekbones and her pouty lips. She was blushing and he realized she must be self-conscious. Elizabeth hoped that he wanted to be here with her and to try to have a normal life again. Then he looked away, unreadable, like a stranger once more.

Chapter Two

The front door opened and the security system chimed an announcement. "Knock, knock," Vie Sonni called out, her smile bright as ever. For a second, Nic's gaze found Elizabeth's, a blank stare on his face. Then the excitement lit him up like a lightbulb as Vie placed Julia in his arms for the first time in months. Her soft black curls were sticking straight up as she laid her head on her dad's chest and grinned up at him. Nic's eyes filled with tears as he ran an awkward hand over the top of his daughter's head. What truly mattered had not changed. Or so Elizabeth wanted to believe.

Elizabeth walked into the well-stocked kitchen and saw Vie unloading two bags of food from Chesca's Restaurant. She stopped to wrap Elizabeth in a hug. "I know you must be tired dear. That's why I brought dinner."

Elizabeth adored Mrs. Vie. She was friendly, fun-loving and active in their church. "Could you be more wonderful?" She thought about all that the elderly lady had done for her – and others in the community. "Don't you have enough to do?"

"I am just grateful that my Walter wasn't injured in the rink." Vie's late husband had also been a hockey player for the New York Islanders and had helped Nic get his start when his family moved to Edgartown.

Vie turned to the sink and turned on the water. "I have got a little bit of time before I have to leave. I might as well make myself useful."

"I have been praying for this for so long, I can't believe he is finally home."

"It puts a different light on the word *blessing*, doesn't it?" Vie asked.

"Yes, it does." Elizabeth's heart filled with gratitude. How easily this moment could have never happened. "Oh, I hear Julia. She is probably getting restless."

"Liz, can you come here?" Nic called out from the living room.

She couldn't be sure that she heard him right. Had he just called her *Liz*?

Elizabeth came to his rescue as Nic held his fatigued little girl. Julia's arms shot up and she thrust herself through the air, trusting her mother would catch her. She wrapped a secure arm around Julia and hefted her onto her hip. She turned her in the direction of the kitchen. "Come on baby, let's go see Mrs. Vie."

One day, she would be sure to pay back Vie for her thoughtfulness. She had been rallying around Elizabeth and pitching in with the child care, laundry – whatever needed to be done. As much as it was appreciated, the weight of the guilt of inconveniencing Vie choked Elizabeth.

"Julia reminds me of my Michel when she was that age." Vie said softly. "Oh, that reminds me. Michel will be coming soon to stay with me here on the island."

"That's nice." Elizabeth sighed and reached in the refrigerator.

"I will let myself out," Vie said before turning to leave.

"Okay, thanks again dear." Elizabeth called out as Vie exited the kitchen.

"I will be praying for you, Nic." Vie said as she patted him on the arm on her way out.

"Thank you." He looked weary as he said it. Elizabeth saw the hurt in his eyes when he turned toward her.

"Vie brought dinner. Do you need help getting to the table?"

"No, I can do it." He put down the photo album he was holding and stood to his feet.

Elizabeth's vision blurred with tears as she watched him toiling forward one slow step at a time. When he reached the table, she laid her hand on his shoulder and she could feel the tension coiled in knots. How difficult this had to be for him. To come home to a house and a family he could not remember. And to see himself in the family photos and realize he wasn't the man he once was. A downside Elizabeth had not anticipated.

The moment she dropped into her chair at the table, she could feel the exhaustion settle over her. "Will you say grace?" she asked. Nic only looked at her bewildered as if he was trying to make sense of her request. When he didn't reply, she answered. "I guess I will." She folded her hands and bowed her head. She asked the blessing over their meal and as she had done every day for the past four weeks, she asked God to heal Nic. Prayer would help. It always did.

"I will help you," she said quietly when she realized Nic's plate remained empty.

He looked away, his stare stone cold. Even though the doctors had been warning her through the long journey of his recovery, she could not accept how everything had changed. There were no more loving looks across the table between them, and no more knowing looks that meant they were storing memories to share with Julia. Other than the occasional clatter of the silverware and the noises that came from having a small child at the dining table, there was just silence. She hadn't realized the importance of the meaningful bond that linked them, until it was gone. Until there was nothing but silence between two strangers, did she realize that the love they had shared was gone too.

When they had finished eating and she had cleaned up the kitchen, Elizabeth turned on the bathwater and adjusted the temperature before adding coconut scented bath salts to the rising water. She slumped down into the Jacuzzi tub and rested her head on the tub wall. Steam swirled around her, causing her straight auburn hair to frizz. But that wasn't what troubled her weary mind. She wondered how the rest of the night would turn out for her and Nic.

She soaked in a warm bath for a few minutes, then rose to her feet and fetched a clean towel from the towel warmer. After putting on her pale blue silk pajamas and matching slippers, she forced her feet forward.

A quick glance into the living room, she found Nic stretched out sound asleep on the sofa with Julia on his chest. Elizabeth made her way over and hit the power off button on the TV remote. She then reached down to pick up her sleeping daughter. Nic didn't stir. The poor man had to be exhausted. Elizabeth lifted the warm fleece blanket off the back of the sofa and gently covered him. She kissed her husband's forehead and prayed in the darkness. *Lord, please help him find his way back to me.*

Chapter Three

"I'm sorry I fell asleep last night."

Elizabeth glanced up from pouring herself a cup of coffee. Nic didn't look at her as he concentrated on stirring the creamer in his coffee.

"It was a big day for all of us, with you coming home."

"But you were dis-disappointed." He blundered on the word as he spoke.

Since she could not admit that, without hurting his feelings, she set the carafe on the table and slipped into the chair next to him. "Were you disappointed?"

Nic stared down into his steaming cup unable to find any answers in the dark depths. Then he gulped as if he were trying to swallow his words. He finally managed to say, "Not really."

On impulse, she rose and plucked her coffee cup from the table. When she turned to walk out of the room, the collage of their wedding photos on the adjacent wall caught her attention. She reached and grabbed it off the wall. When she tried to lay it on the table, Nic moved his cup aside to make room. As he studied the photographs, she leaned in over his shoulder. She could smell the scent of his cologne that she'd given him on their anniversary, causing her pulse to race.

He touched his hand to the photo where they stood hand in hand as husband and wife. "You look happy."

"I was. It was one of the best days of my life," she replied. Their happiness was palpable, evidence of their love for one another.

"I look happy, too."

"Yes, you were." "I wish you could remember how it felt to be married in front of our family and friends."

She noticed the sadness on his face and the wonder in his eyes. It wasn't fair that the accident had taken so much from him. At least she had the memories of their love. But she was beginning to wonder if that was enough.

How did she tell him that was her biggest fear? That they might never find the love they had for one another again. That they might never share that close bond they'd had. Grief stabbed deep into her heart. She had to somehow keep her faith and believe that God would not forsake them.

She retreated to the kitchen, taking the carafe with her to rinse in the sink. But everywhere she looked, even on the refrigerator door, were photos of a happier time when Nic was whole. It was not fair to keep wishing for the past she thought as she rinsed the carafe and slipped it into the dishwasher. She closed the dishwasher quietly, as reality settled into the broken parts of her heart.

"I will take care of you. I'll help you to remember," she promised Nic as he walked into the room.

He nodded, but he did not look as if he believed her.

There was the quick tap-tap of Vie's signature knock on the front door. Her key was already in the lock and she was turning the knob. The security system chimed its notification as the door swung open. "Hello. Is anybody home?" Vie's jovial voice echoed in the foyer.

"Come on in. We are in the kitchen." Elizabeth's voice was drowned out by the cries coming from Julia's room.

"I'll get her." Nic announced.

Elizabeth's eyes widened with concern. "Are you sure?"

He stared at her, but he did not say anything at all. For him it was a matter of pride.

"What time is Nic's appointment?" Vie asked, pulling Elizabeth's attention from Nic as he shuffled down the hallway towards Julia's bedroom.

"It is at ten o'clock." Elizabeth glanced at the time on her cell phone. "We need to be leaving soon."

"I will take care of Julia while you are gone. And have lunch ready when you get back."

Elizabeth let out a sigh of relief. She was deeply grateful. "Thank you, Mrs. Vie. I don't know how I will ever repay you for all that you have done."

"No worries, dear. That is why I'm here."

Nic ambled back into the room toward Elizabeth but his gaze was fixed on their daughter. The little girl's brown eyes widened with exhilaration when she spotted her mother across the room. Nic leaned forward as he handed Julia off to Elizabeth. When her daughter looked up at her, she smiled, tugging at Elizabeth's heart strings.

"Everything is going to work out," she told her, certain of it now.

Chapter Four

"I brought my toolbox," Justen Ben-David, clad in a navy T-shirt and faded denims, said in his raspy voice as he sauntered through the front door and stomped his boots on the entry rug. "Thought Nic and I could get a few things done around here."

Elizabeth looked up. "Hi Justen!" she said to Nic's younger brother. She could not have a better brother-in-law and she was grateful he wanted to help out, but she wasn't sure that Nic was up to the challenge. "We can worry about things getting done around here later."

"You know me. I am not happy unless I am working on something." He winked and his smile was good-natured as always. Elizabeth was surprised that he hadn't found a woman who could look past the gruff exterior to the sweet man on the inside.

"And how are you doing?" he asked.

"I'm doing well." She smiled to prove it, but judging by the squint to his dark brown eyes, he was not fooled one bit.

"Is Nic resting?" he quizzed.

"Yes, he fell asleep on the sofa after we ate lunch. He had an appointment with his doctor this morning."

"What did doc have to say?"

"It was just a routine follow-up. The doctor said that it was common for people with memory loss to remember somethings, but not others," Elizabeth answered. "Can I get you something to drink, Justen?"

"A glass of milk would be great! And I'll take one of these brownies. They smell delicious!"

Elizabeth poured him a glass of milk and joined him at the counter. Justen was smiling as he tore into the brownie. "No one makes a better brownie than you." A compliment, but one she'd heard before. Plus Justen was generous with compliments.

"You can watch TV in the game room if you don't want to disturb Nic."

"Oh, I don't mind bothering Nic!" Justen winked as he strode out of the kitchen. The faint mumble of his voice in the living room told her that Nic must have woken up.

When she peered around the corner to check on him, he had straightened up on the sofa. Now sitting up, he and Justen were both smiling and talking like old friends. He seemed to remember his brother. Elizabeth saw the hurt in his eyes when he looked toward her. How could he remember Justen but not her?

She blew out a deep breath and went back to the kitchen. The men's voices rumbled throughout the house as she finished preparing the salad for dinner. She remembered how it used to be. How Nic would hang around the kitchen while she cooked dinner, grazing on whatever was handy to snack on. The oven timer beeped at that moment. She hit the off button and grabbed an over-sized oven mitt from the closest drawer. She lifted the casserole from the oven and onto a trivet on the counter. While she overheard Nic and Justen talking, she tried not to focus on the words.

Her heart was heavy. Somehow she had to find a way to lay aside her anger. Surely there was some good that would come out of this – some good that the Lord would bring out of this hardship. But right now Elizabeth couldn't figure out what that may be.

It was Nic's voice, low and resonant, that made her stop halfway to the living room. "Yes, I do remember that," he was saying. Nic noticed her standing there and it was hard for her to tell by the look on his face if he was happy to see her or not. When he looked at her, he had to feel pressure to remember the life they had shared.

Justen turned in his seat and looked at her. "I'm going to take Nic with me."

Nic's eyes widened in surprise. "Where are we going?" Perhaps he didn't remember that Justen was always eager to work on things.

"Justen, Nic is still recuperating. But he can go with you and keep you company."

"Sure!" Justen nodded once and rose to his feet as if that were settled. "What do you say, big brother?

"Count me in!" Nic stood to his feet and hope glinted in his big brown eyes and his lopsided smile could not be bigger. "I'll return soon, Liz."

Liz! He never called her that before the accident. Had he somehow re-invented her in his mind? Had he conjured up an image of who he *wanted* her to be?

"You better be back in time for dinner, both of you!" Elizabeth called out as they neared the door.

"You got it!" exclaimed Justen. "We won't be long."

While the guys were off doing whatever it was they were doing, Vie and her daughter, Michel, arrived at the house. With her sleek blond hair, girl-next-door smile and great clothes sense, Michel was gorgeous. And thin. Elizabeth thought that she paled by comparison.

Over the noise at the dinner table, Elizabeth heard Vie lean over to Nic and ask, "How is it that you're so handsome?"

A blush emphasized his cheeks, making him even better-looking to Elizabeth.

"Guess I'm just lucky!"

That made Vie chuckle in that joyful way of hers.

Elizabeth looked up from her plate, and her heart raced. Could it be that he was remembering? Nic always used to say that. *Guess I'm just lucky.* Wouldn't it be remarkable if he did defy the doctor's grim prognoses? As she scanned everyone seated at the table, she saw nothing but amusement and love mixed together in a way that only God could do.

Vie's cheerful voice broke into her thoughts. "Nic, don't you worry about not remembering things. You are not alone dear. It happens to me all the time!"

Everyone chuckled, trying to make light of the situation.

"So, you don't remember where you and Elizabeth met?" Michel asked, turning the mood somber once again.

"No, I do not," he answered solemnly.

Elizabeth read the shame on her husband's face. "Vie likes to think she's the reason we're together."

Nic raised his thick brow, "Is that so?"

The elderly woman chuckled warmly. "Your marriage is a testimony to the power of prayer. My husband, Walter, was still with me back then. We had already met young Elizabeth and wanted her to have a happy marriage like ours. So I decided to start praying to the Lord for her a good man – strong, yet gentle and loving."

"You had just come into town," Elizabeth explained, remembering that summer they'd met. She felt the cold places within her warm like that hot July day. He nodded in acknowledgment, but not in understanding. She longed for him to remember her and how they met. She wished he could remember how blue the sky was and how vibrant he had looked with the ocean behind him.

Nic looked puzzled as he gave her that lopsided grin. Elizabeth smiled, unable to find words to describe how deeply she had fallen for him. Before she could continue on, Vie chimed in from across the table, "Did I mention that I had to resort to prayer?" She had to laugh at herself, fighting against the pull of sadness. How could he not remember the love of his life? How could so much be wiped clean like chalk from a chalkboard?

Elizabeth reached out and laid her hand on Nic's. Gone was the connection she had once felt to him; the bond between their two hearts. She ached remembering the excitement of their first date and the endless possibilities. She closed her hand around his and he seemed to tighten his grip as if to say he wasn't going to let her go. But Nic wasn't looking at her; his gaze was affixed across the table on Michel.

Later, after everyone was gone, and Julia was bathed and in her bed, Elizabeth was alone with Nic. She eased onto the posh sofa next to him. In an instant, the memory of their first meeting came back to her with all of its feelings and array of vivid images. The heat of the afternoon sun warmed her skin. She could feel the whoosh of the wind in her long auburn hair and the uneven brick pathway beneath her feet. She could recall how the gleeful squawk of seagulls carried on the gentle breeze. But all of that had faded when she first glimpsed the tall, wide-shouldered man standing on the pier. It had been love at first sight. But now, even with her memories and all the love she held in her heart for him, the connection they had shared was not there.

Chapter Five

After much thought, Elizabeth had decided that the two of them needed a date night. How long had it been? It was hard to think back that far, past the fog since his accident, to when life had been normal. It had been busy and hectic, but normal. Maybe going on a date would help his memory. Hope rose up within her once more.

Elizabeth glanced up and noticed the expression on her husband's face. She might not know what he was thinking, but he was clearly amused. She also noticed something else. Did that smile on his face mean that he was happy?

She leaned in closer to him. "We should go on a date!" she announced.

"But we're married."

"Yes, but we used to go out every Friday night, just the two of us. We could go your favorite restaurant."

"*My favorite restaurant?*" Humor flashed in Nic's eyes. "Woman, you could take me anywhere and I would never know the difference!"

Elizabeth laughed aloud, feeling more at ease than she had in a long time. She winked at him. "That didn't occur to me. Thanks for pointing that out!" Her heart fluttered with anticipation the way it had before their first date.

She was determined and resolute that everything was going to be okay. She was going to have her husband back and Julia would have her father again. *It had to be okay.* She didn't know if her heart could take more hardship.

"I will see if Vie can watch Julia for a couple of hours. If so, we are on for Friday night," she declared.

Nic turned to look at her. "It doesn't seem like I have a say in the matter."

In the blink of an eye, the hurt and anger that she thought had diminished reared its ugly head. She did her best to rub out any doubt that existed beneath her resolve, and to cling to her faith. Sadness filled her as she looked into his eyes and realized how hard this had to be for him. To be bereft of all the memories that had made up his life – their life.

The sunshine had chosen that moment to shine through the window in rich, jeweled tones, spilling over Nic. And seeing him in those gallant colors; it was like an answer to her prayers. She had to find a way to push aside all her anger and have a positive outlook for Nic's sake.

"Will you tell me about our first date?" He asked, watching her with unblinking eyes.

Her memory of their first date was keen but she could not muster the words to speak. There was so much to say, and so much that couldn't be put into words. Love was like that, it could only be felt.

Nic reached out for her hand. His movements were slow, his touch gentle, as he wrapped her hand with his. His gaze was full of emotion and tenderness. "Help me remember, Liz."

She hadn't given up hope when he was in the hospital, when his survival had been nothing more than a small chance and she wouldn't give up on him now.

Julia cried out from her bedroom. It took some effort for Elizabeth to withdraw her hand from Nic's but she had to check on their daughter. As she made her way down the hall, she said a silent prayer. "Thank you, Lord."

Elizabeth scooped up her daughter, who had Nic's dark brown eyes and frothy black hair, and snuggled the sleepy child close. Julia's favorite teddy bear was tucked in the crook of her arm as she carried her to the living room. Nic looked up as she entered the room. "Do you mind watching her while I prepare lunch? It's only pizza, but it'll be piping hot and on the table in a few minutes."

He sighed reluctantly, but replied, "No, not at all."

Elizabeth handed Julia off to him and made her way to the kitchen. She had been spending far more time in there than she was accustomed to. She looked forward to the day she could return to her work as a photographer. The island would soon be thriving with tourists and the families who spent their summers on Martha's Vineyard. Emotion balled up in her throat. Battling down the emotions, she ripped open the cardboard box and slid the frozen pizza onto a big cookie sheet.

In the other room, Julia studied her father's face as if seeing him for the first time. As young as she was, she knew there was something different about the father who'd come home to her. From where she stood in the kitchen, Elizabeth could see the hurt on Nic's face. But he held his daughter quietly, not willing to risk a meltdown of sorts.

Within a few minutes, Elizabeth's announcement rang out from the kitchen. "The pizza is ready!" Not exactly the healthiest meal, but definitely comfort food. The kind she was in the mood for.

"Liz, can you come get her?" Nic pleaded.

Why does he insist on calling me Liz? She mumbled to herself.

"Sure, I will be right there!"

Julia clapped her small hands together with glee as Elizabeth crossed the living room floor toward her. Air caught in Elizabeth's lungs as her daughter gazed up at her with awe on her face. Elizabeth reached down and hefted her on her hip, then kissed her soft, rose-colored cheek.

Watching Julia with Elizabeth, Nic felt like a stranger, an outsider. He was only now seeing how impossible it was to get back what he had lost. He'd lost time with each of them, precious time that was gone forever. Unbearable anger surged through him like the sharp edge of a knife. He exhaled, realizing he was shaking with uncontrollable feelings which he didn't know how to deal with. His gaze was drawn to a professionally framed and matted picture of a snow-covered evergreen. It was a collector's piece with a numbered tag tucked into the frame. Hebrews 11:1, *"Now faith is confidence in what we hope for and assurance about what we do not see"*, was written in the corner, beneath a familiar signature.

Elizabeth's voice filled his ears and his thoughts. "The pizza is getting cold."

Nic had to clear the emotion from his throat before he could speak. "I'm on my way." He pasted a smile on his face as he rose to his feet.

As he made his way to the dining room table, Nic took in the neat and tidy kitchen. Elizabeth had done more than prepare a pizza; she had washed the breakfast dishes, and sorted through the mail that had accumulated on the counter. Even in his dilapidated condition, he could see that the Lord had blessed him with a good woman, a woman he must have once loved.

Chapter Six

Nic took the photo album marked *Our Wedding* off the shelf as he waited for Elizabeth to finish getting dressed for their date. He prayed for a lot of things these days, but he didn't pray for himself, he prayed for her. *Lord, please help me to remember for her sake.*

He fought to find a single scrap of recognition in the professional quality photographs of the two of them smiling, hand in hand, their gold wedding rings glistening.

Elizabeth's picture stared back at him. Her face was younger, softer; untouched by the fine lines of worry that his injury and the loss of his career had carved there. He would give anything to be able to make things right. From the moment he'd woken from the coma she had been by his side. He turned the page, stopping to listen to her voice that carried down the hallway. She was talking with Vie, who had arrived to stay with Julia.

He wondered if Elizabeth had known what was down the road for her, would she still have married him anyway. Failure nipped at him, and he closed the photo album and set in on the coffee table. The accident had changed the course of their lives and he feared that old life was gone for good.

Elizabeth – Liz, as Nic called her – swept into the living room wearing a knee length black dress that made her look so beautiful that he could not believe his eyes. He rose to his feet, wishing he was the man he used to be. She grabbed her purse as she escorted him in the direction of the door. Vie and Elizabeth exchanged emotional looks, as if in silent understanding.

"Enjoy your evening!" Vie called out as Elizabeth held the door patiently as Nic walked through. Her reply echoed briefly through the doorway before the door clicked shut.

Everything in Nic longed to love this woman who opened the passenger door for him and didn't look at him as less of a man for having done so. His heart ached in all the empty places where he supposed his love for her used to be. He wished he could remember one thing about her and then maybe he wouldn't feel as if he were with an acquaintance instead of the woman he had married.

"Are you hungry?" She smiled up at him as he settled into the seat.

"Where are we going?" he asked.

"I know you won't remember, but it is where we went on our first date. They have the best steak and seafood in town."

Some of the ever-present tension washed from his face as he admitted, "That sounds good!"

Once they were seated inside of Atlantic Fish & Chop House, Elizabeth looked over the top of the menu at her husband seated across the table from her. His puzzled expression morphed into a shy grin.

"Don't order the Chilean Sea Bass," she reminded him, forgetting that he wouldn't know that it was an inside joke.

"Sea Bass?" he repeated, as he searched the menu for the words. When he spotted it on the menu, he tapped the picture with his index finger. "Oh, I see the Chilean Sea Bass."

"You usually ordered the filet mignon, cooked medium rare, with a Caesar salad," Elizabeth stated.

"That does sound good! I am not so sure I want to be reminded about the Sea Bass." He chuckled and for a moment he was like the old Nic, the one she knew so well. The one she missed talking to and sharing with.

The waitress chose that moment to stop at their table. It was Michel. Elizabeth watched as a smile crept onto Nic's face. "How nice to see you two," Michel greeted them.

"I did not expect to see you here." Elizabeth replied, matter-of-factly.

"I love mom, don't get me wrong, but I had to find a part-time job for the summer. I would go stir crazy if I had to stay home with her every day!" Michel confessed.

Nic watched the puzzlement creep onto Elizabeth's face and so he gave a shrug.

"What appetizer can I start you off with?"

"We will start with the Escargot Parisienne," Elizabeth replied.

Michel wrote it down, along with their drink orders, and then sauntered away.

Nic and Elizabeth sat in silence, and the distance between them felt vast. She had not noticed it before, at least not like this. She sat face-to-face with him without the medical staff or Julia to interrupt them. Conversation had always flowed easily between them, but now it felt as if she was sitting with a stranger.

"Nic!" Erik Whitmore exclaimed as he approached the table. "Sorry to interrupt. It is good to see you out and about!"

"No problem. It may be good for Nic to see you, as well." Elizabeth replied.

Nic rubbed his temple with his hand. "Sorry, but I don't think I know you."

Elizabeth reached across the table for Nic's hand. Her gesture was so sincere that his heart broke all over again. She had touched him in comfort, with love. "Nic, this is one of your former teammates, Erik Whitmore."

Nic looked bewildered, but reached out to shake the man's hand. "Nice to meet you," he said, as if meeting Erik for the first time.

"I just thought I would come over and say hello. Just wanted to let you know we are praying for you."

"Thanks, Erik." Elizabeth gave a courteous smile.

Nic reached to shake the man's hand once more. "Sorry I don't remember you."

"No worries. Enjoy the rest of your evening." Erik gave a nod and went back to his table.

Elizabeth watched Nic's face carefully as he rubbed his temples again. Was there a glimmer of a memory; something familiar just out of reach? She simply had to keep believing. Keep trusting that God would bring them together again. Gratitude filled her and she found it easy to smile as Michel returned to deliver their drinks and the Escargot Parisienne they had ordered. As the evening progressed, Elizabeth and Nic made small talk as they ate dinner.

Elizabeth navigated the Range Rover along the main road that led from the restaurant to the oceanfront. She pulled into the nearly empty gravel lot. Only a few utility vehicles were parked, awaiting their owners. Nic studied the view of the ocean. "This is a beautiful place."

"Yes it is." Elizabeth turned off the engine and grabbed her keys from the ignition. "Do you remember coming here?"

He shook his head, as if to say no. There was so much for him to remember; a lot of water under the bridge of their lives.

"Do you feel up to a short walk?" she asked, hoping their love of the ocean view would somehow trigger some memories.

"Sure. I guess so."

The evening sun, setting on the horizon, cast a shadow on her face as she circled around the Range Rover to the passenger side. Nothing felt better than being here, with Nic. Joy lifted her up as if she were floating on a cloud. Yet she found herself at a loss for words, not knowing what to say to him.

They shuffled forward on the resistive brick walkway. "I want you to remember me!" she cried out. Maybe it was selfish, she didn't know, but she had never felt lonelier at her husband's side.

He nodded as if in understanding, but the strong line of his jaw hardened. They continued to walk in silence; it was easier for him that way.

Elizabeth studied her husband's face. He seemed to have something on his mind. He did not stop her as she covered his hand with hers. Touching him dragged up more loneliness from her soul. How could she begin to explain to him how lonely she was for him? For his kiss, his strong arms to hold her?

"Do you love me?" her heart ached as she asked the question. She did not think she could handle hearing the answer *no*, even if it were the honest answer.

"What?" He looked into her sad eyes. "I can see the stress this has caused you." He tore his gaze away from her, staring out into space, causing her heart to break a little more. Why had their wonderful lives been shattered in the first place? She had to remind herself that it was not God's doing, but a desperate man's – a man with free will.

"All of this has not been easy for me, Nic. But it is nothing compared to what you have been through. I only want to make things better for you. I am supposed to take care of you."

He nodded. "And you have done a good job." He struggled not to show any emotion, but she could sense that he was keeping something hidden from her.

"Nic, I love you," she said, hoping somehow it would change something between them.

His jaw trembled as he spoke, "I can see that. I just can't say the same about you. I'm sorry, Liz." He saw the pain on her face and he felt it in his heart. As hurtful as it may have been, that was how it was.

"Oh, Nic, please don't do this."

"You need more than I can give you," he replied.

"I need you, Nic. I don't care about how things are. How you are." Tears burned in her eyes, but she could not look away from him. She took a wobbly step, emotion catching in her throat as she did her best to explain. "I never stopped believing in you. I never stopped having faith that you would open your eyes. That is why I stayed by your side, so that when you woke up, you were not alone. And I don't want you to leave me now."

A muscle tightened in his jaw, but he said nothing. He looked as if he couldn't.

"No matter what you decide, you have my love," she spoke softly.

Deep with emotion, his voice carried through the cool air. "Liz, I think we should see other people."

"Are you saying that you want a divorce?" she asked, in disbelief. In the silence, she hung her head, waiting, knowing Nic would only speak the truth to her. And knowing that he could not say and feel what she needed him to.

Finally, he broke the silence. "Yes… yes, I guess that is what I'm trying to say." It was clear to him that they were not emotionally connected the way they used to be. Despite time spent together, she was still a stranger to him.

Her body trembled as waves of hurt washed over her. Her sobs were uncontrollable, but he did nothing to comfort her. He didn't know how.

Chapter Seven

Elizabeth was in the hallway when she heard Julia crying out from her bedroom. Memories clung to her like the shadow on the wall. Images of before Nic had been injured. Of Nic quietly checking on their sleeping daughter, adoration shining off him as he carefully shut the door. Of how he would smile and wink at her, knowing they could be alone once Julia was asleep. Tears filled her eyes and she tried to blink them away. The empty hallway stared back at her, and she heard Julia's faint cry. She brushed back the sting from her eyes. She just wanted their lives to be put back together again. It would take some time, but that was all she had.

Elizabeth pulled out a chair and collapsed into it. She concluded that she was more tired than she'd thought. Looking at Julia's sweet face put a smile on her's but caused throbs of pain in her chest. The break up with Nic had been hard on Elizabeth. She groaned as her cell phone rang. Vie's home number was on the screen.

"Hello?" she answered with what she hoped sounded like an enthusiastic greeting.

"Hi dear, it is Vie. How are you?"

"I am doing okay," Elizabeth replied. "And how are you?"

"Oh, I am doing well dear. Thanks for asking. I was down at the bookstore this morning and Spencer said that he is shorthanded. I told him that I would ask you if you wanted to work. He is lonely, too, you know. That is why he works such long hours at the bookstore."

"Is that so?" Elizabeth asked, hoping to keep the conversation on Spencer and off of her.

She sighed and thought about how the extra income would help out as Vie continued on about Spencer's love life or lack thereof. Finally, she interrupted Vie. "Let me think about it. Can I get back with you?"

"Just let Spencer know what you decide. He definitely needs the help." Vie replied. "You know I will be happy to keep Julia for you," she added before ending the call.

Elizabeth felt oddly alone as she headed to the kitchen. "This too shall pass." she said aloud as she entered the empty room. As she went around tidying up the kitchen and getting ready for the day, she listened to the low murmur of Julia's coos and giggles floating serenely around the house.

She made her way into the living room where she found Julia in her swing. The little girl with the sleep-tousled curly hair and Cinderella pajamas gazed up with total adoration at her mother. Elizabeth ran her hand, gentle and loving, over the crown of her daughter's head. "I love you, baby girl," she announced cheerfully and Julia looked joyful. For once Elizabeth's memories of the past and her hope for the future were not one and the same.

Once Julia was securely fastened in her car seat, Elizabeth jumped in behind the steering wheel. She clicked her seat belt into place and said a silent prayer as the Range Rover rolled out of the driveway. *Lord, show me the way. Show me how to take care of this incredible blessing You have given me.* As they made the drive into town to Edgartown Bookstore, Elizabeth glanced in the rearview mirror with tenderness on her face. She was truly grateful for her daughter.

With Julia on her hip, Elizabeth made her way through the doorway of the bookstore. A vase of fragrant, white Calla Lilies greeted her senses as she entered inside. It was hard not to remember her wedding since her choice of flowers had been the same. She recalled seeing Nic standing at the altar, watching for her to come down the aisle, and how his face had lit up with awe when he saw her in her wedding dress for the first time. The dress had been beautiful. She had it still, wrapped carefully and stored in her closet.

When she reached the end of the aisle, there he was. Nic was standing there talking with Michel Sonni. He was smiling, nothing except polite interest on his face. But when he turned around to see Elizabeth standing there, not a single drop of recognition showed on his face.

"Elizabeth! Hi. You look great." Michel said, smiling at her.

Elizabeth shifted Julia to her other hip and lowered her gaze to the floor. "Hi," was all she could bring herself to say when she walked by.

Michel was the epitome of happiness as she stood there talking and laughing like old friends with Nic. She tilted her head when she laughed, silky blond hair cascading down her back. Nic looked handsome in his navy blue pullover shirt and khakis. Elizabeth's love for him drew her to him like a rope pulling her forward. But then he and Michel turned and headed down the aisle together.

Her stomach fluttered with nerves. Perhaps she shouldn't take the job. Better yet, she probably shouldn't have come here in the first place. She ambled across the crowded room and stopped, Spencer's gaze finding hers. For once, in a long time, a smile brightened her face, her eyes, and her soul.

The telephone in the bookstore rang, and as Spencer leaned to pick it up he kept his amazing blue eyes on Elizabeth. He could not rightly say why his heart stirred, but it did. He gave her a grin as he put his ear to the receiver. "Hello?" Elizabeth's eyes flickered cheerfully over the top of Julia's curls. Hope welled up in her chest, making it hard for her to breathe.

Spencer could not look away. His eyes refused to move. His heartbeat stalled, leaving only a quiver of emotion too tender to name. He longed for this moment to last and for the chance to reach out and touch the sleekness of her auburn hair. He ached to pull her into the shelter of his arms. Then she looked away and the moment was broken. His pulse thumped to life again, and his troubles returned.

Chapter Eight

I want you to remember me. Elizabeth's plea still troubled Nic. It whispered to him every morning when he opened his eyes and again before he closed them at night. It tore him up every time he ran into her up town. He wondered what or who it was that made her so happy these days. In talking with others around town, he had learned that the two of them had been best friends, just as Elizabeth had said.

Nic thought of the vacation photos he had studied and how his daughter had been in his arms in nearly every photograph. He thought of the way Julia had been gazing up at him with such love and need. Emotion welled up in his chest, making every beat of his heart hurt.

He tried to recall why he had made the decision to let them go. And then he remembered when people had asked how he was adjusting to being home, he usually replied, "Just fine," because more times than not, Elizabeth had been at his side. He hadn't wanted her to hear the truth. The way she had looked at him with those big blue eyes of hers was so sad and hopeful at the same time. It was agonizing to think he was letting her down. Just fine *had* been the truth, just not the whole truth. He was doing fine except he did not know his own wife and daughter, and was trying to live a life that did not feel like it belonged to him.

The past was gone, whether Nic remembered it or not. It could never be resurrected or relived. And if his memories of the past never returned, that did not mean that it had to change the course of their lives, of their commitment to one another. He wanted Liz, his wife, his best friend back. He prayed to the Lord that it wasn't too late.

It was nearly twilight as Elizabeth carried Julia on her hip and followed the wraparound porch along the side of Nic's house. She inhaled deeply and realized she was at peace. The hurt and worries that plagued her after their divorce had vanished. No doubt they had been replaced by other ones, since that was the way life seemed to go. Then she turned the corner and saw Nic staring out at the beautiful ocean.

"Want some company?" It may not be the best timing, she thought as she approached him.

He did not startle; he must have heard them coming.

"I thought you'd never get here," he teased.

They smiled together. "Your sense of humor was one of the things I loved most about you." Elizabeth admitted.

"Not my dashing good looks?"

"I don't think you are good-looking, but a girl can't have it all," she teased, barely able to keep from laughing because it was far from the truth.

That made Nic laugh, a deep rumbling sound of joy. He shook his head. "I guess I asked for that one!"

When Elizabeth was seated next to Nic, he reached for Julia and placed her onto his lap. Over the top of their daughter's frothy curls, there was no mistaking the joy in his eyes.

After a few minutes had passed, she asked, "Why don't you tell me why you are out here all by yourself?"

"I am just tired," he answered.

But there was more to it than that, she knew by the lines on his face and the silence that once again settled between them. As expected, Nic's frown hardened into a grimace. He turned away, staring at a seagull circling above the nearby pier.

She reached out and rested her hand on his shoulder. Relief eased his tense shoulders. Nic turned toward her and laid his arm along the back of the bench, not exactly hugging her, but close enough. Just as he had done on their first date. Elizabeth leaned back, delighting in just being with him. With Julia still seated on his lap, he leaned a little closer to her. It felt as if they were more than just physically closer. Tears scalded the back of her eyes. She swallowed hard, to push them away.

Footsteps rang out on the wooden porch boards behind them, pounding closer. It was Spencer. The moment between Elizabeth and Nic was lost, but not the hope.

The awkwardness of that moment left Elizabeth speechless as she looked up at Spencer. "I didn't expect to see you here, he barked." No smile, but that was Spencer, tough on the outside and kind hearted on the inside. She could see the strain on his face, the deep-set lines and how disappointed he looked. Worry shook her and automatically she turned to look at Nic, her gaze fastening on his. Unlike old times, he did not instantly know what she meant without words. But he did enfold her hand with his.

Spencer rubbed the back of his neck. "I guess I came at a bad time." His ominous tone made her fret just a little. Neither she nor Nic had a chance to reply. Spencer was already walking away, pulling his keys out of his front pants pocket.

Nic seemed proud as he gazed at his daughter, who was joyfully clapping her hands with a grin on her sweet face. Julia was pleased that she had her parent's attention. "That's our little girl," Nic whispered to Elizabeth. "She is ours." She heard what he didn't say. She felt it with her heart. Their daughter had been conceived from the love they had shared. And now Elizabeth had to be patient and trust where God was leading them.

Chapter Nine

After a quick stop at Morrice Florist the next morning, Elizabeth headed straight to Martha's Vineyard Hospital, the same one where Nic had stayed for four grueling weeks. She had gone there so many times the Range Rover could probably drive itself. She pulled into visitor parking, grabbed her Lily Pulitzer purse and the bouquet of cheerful flowers and headed toward the hospital entrance.

As she walked the somber halls, her mind flashed back to that horrible night. The tap, tap of her heels echoed in the bleak long halls. The antiseptic and sadness in the air made her mouth go dry. She had walked down a corridor just like this one on her way to see Nic in ICU for the first time. She had prayed so hard then, and she prayed now for Vie's sake.

"Elizabeth! Over here." Michel poked her head out of a doorway and waved. She looked as beautiful as ever with her blond hair flowing over her shoulder and her big blue eyes sparkling. "Mom had a sudden rise in blood pressure, but she is all right now. They are sending her home today."

"Wow! That is good…"

Michel interrupted her. "How are things with you and Nic? I heard that the two of you were dating again."

"We have gone out a few times."

Eager to change the subject, Michel quipped, "You should probably take those flowers to the house, since mom is being released."

Despite what Michel had said, Elizabeth glanced around the room then shuffled a few vases on the windowsill to make room for her cheerful floral arrangement.

"Good morning dear." Vie chimed in, her arms wide, to give Elizabeth a hug. She looked pale and tired, but other than that, she looked good. Michel was now at her mother's bedside, holding her wrinkled hand.

"How are you feeling?" Elizabeth asked the elderly woman.

"I am perky compared to yesterday." Vie managed a sweet smile. "Thanks for the flowers. They are lovely!"

"You will feel even better when you are back at home." Elizabeth reassured her.

"I will make sure she takes her medication," Michel stated, a little forcefully.

Vie glanced around the room, as if she were confused, then nodded to her daughter.

"I have been pitching in whenever the staffing situation is dire at the bookstore." Elizabeth said before her phone rang, its electronic tune muffled by her purse. She fished it from her Lilly Pulitzer purse and saw Nic's cell phone number on the screen. "Excuse me," she said over her shoulder, heading toward the door. "Hello?"

"Hi, babe!" Nic's baritone voice never sounded quite so good. "Justen just showed up here. He needs some help with a project this afternoon but I wanted to check with you, and see if you needed me to watch Julia."

Unexpected tears burned her eyes. To think that he had called her, to see if she needed him to care for their daughter, tied her up in inexplicable knots. And his memory seemed to be improving by the day. She had to stop wishing for what they had lost and be grateful for what they had now.

"No, that will be fine. But I do appreciate you checking with me, Nic." She hoped her voice sounded normal and not strained with emotion. "I'll meet you at your house later this evening."

"Good. I look forward to seeing you."

Elizabeth's heart filled at the sincerity of his words. She could picture him in her mind, standing so stalwart, a stronger man for all the hardship he had been through and endured. She could hardly wait to see him again.

She walked back inside the hospital room to say her goodbyes to Vie and Michel before heading to the bookstore. Julia was with a sitter since Elizabeth had promised Spencer that she would help out for a few hours today.

As she eased the Range Rover into the parking lot, she couldn't help but notice the shiny, silver convertible Mercedes already parked there. Envious, Elizabeth smiled to herself as she shut the engine off and made her way inside of the bookstore.

Spencer was vaguely aware of her bustling in the door as he chatted with the slender black haired beauty standing in front of him. Elizabeth's jaw dropped when she realized who the woman was. *Sue Deveraux*!

"Hi there, Elizabeth," Carly called out from behind the counter. "I'm glad you could come in for a few hours. It's time for Jacob's checkup. Can you believe he is already six months old?"

"Yes, time flies," Elizabeth nodded. She stood a little straighter, and then asked, "What is Sue Deveraux doing here? I thought she moved away."

"I think she moved to Florida. But she has a new book out called *Opt to Adopt*. She is doing a book signing here this afternoon." Carly replied as her cell phone rang. "Excuse me," she called out over her shoulder, heading toward the door.

Sue's movements were like poetry as she pulled copies of her book from the oversized designer tote bag, each movement graceful and deliberate. The sweet scent of her Chanel perfume or the classical music that was softly playing in the background was things Spencer might forget, but not her. He had been rendered speechless by the sight of her, dressed in an immaculate black dress and six inch heels. Now watching her in the simple act of opening the books and brushing her perfectly manicured fingertips across the pages, he was fascinated by her. By the small smile on her lips, by the glitter of happiness in her eyes, and by her posture so effortless that he could not stop watching her.

"Here are the invoices that I've been working on." Elizabeth announced, drawing Spencer's attention from the curvaceous woman standing nearby.

"Thanks, Elizabeth." His smile faded. "You have been a big help around here!"

"My pleasure. Let me know if you need anything else, okay?"

"Yes, I will." Then he turned and walked away.

Elizabeth watched Spencer during the course of the afternoon as he eyed Sue across the room, chatting with customers as she signed copies of her book. Could it be that he did, in fact, have a genuine interest in Sue Deveraux?

Chapter Ten

Elizabeth pulled the camera out of her closet, not even remembering how it had gotten in there. When was the last time she used it? Oh, for Julia's first birthday party. The laughter from the backyard drifting through the open window reminded her that better times had come back to them. Justen and Michel had made their way over. And Spencer had accepted their invitation to come over, but as it turned out, he wasn't alone. Sue was seated next to him when his Toyota truck pulled into the driveway.

With camera in hand, she checked the battery. It was not dead but it was low. She went back through the closet looking for the plug-in. Sitting next to it on the shelf were half-done scrapbook pages she kept meaning to finish. She brought them out onto her work desk.

Her cell phone rang, echoing through the house. With camera and charger in one hand, she answered the phone with her other. "Hello?"

"Elizabeth?" Vie's voice came across the line, sounding much stronger. "You left me a message dear and I'm finally getting back to you."

"You've been on my mind and in my prayers. I just wanted to see how you were doing."

"Oh, I am doing better." Vie replied, in her usual chipper tone.

"Would you like to come over? Nic and Justen are putting some steaks on the grill as we speak."

"Why, yes, I think I would like that. Thanks for the invite dear. I'll see you soon."

"Okay, see you soon." Elizabeth hung up. Her gaze went to the wide window and the backyard. With his black hair tousled by the wind, Nic looked more like the man she had fallen in love with. He looked to be giving advice to younger brother Justen. And Julia was running around, giggling with excitement. The blissful sounds drifted in like the sunlight and made her heart ache with gratitude.

Elizabeth took the camera with her on the way to the backyard. She watched from the shade beneath the overhead deck as Nic reached down and scooped Julia in his strong arms when she ran by. She squealed with delight. Elizabeth lifted the camera, flipped off the lens cover and captured the image forever.

Nic knelt to whisper something in his daughter's ear. Side by side, it was easy to see how much she resembled her father. She had his smile and his dimpled cheeks. Without hesitation, Elizabeth lifted the camera to capture the image of Nic and Julia, hand in hand.

"Mommy!" Julia called out when she spotted her mother walking towards them.

Nic reached out his hand, his fingertips grazing Elizabeth's cheek. There was tenderness in his touch as he caressed her skin. "You are the most beautiful woman in the world to me." After all their years together, she did not know exactly what he saw when he looked at her. "Oh, Nic," she blushed at his compliment.

"Now more than ever, babe, you and Julia are my world."

Her love for Nic was like an ocean wave crashing against the shore and washing away her doubts and her fears. "I love you, Nic."

"Hello!" a woman's voice called out. Julia shrieked with excitement, racing over to the open gate where Vie stood in a pair of khaki shorts and a nautical themed shirt. She reached out her hand to pat the little girl's head. "Hello, princess! I have missed you."

"We had better go rescue Mrs. Vie," Elizabeth said teasingly. Nic twined his fingers with hers and they made their way over to welcome their neighbor, who was already surrounded by Julia and their other guests.

After they had finished eating dinner, Elizabeth and Vie were doing the cleanup while the others were outside. Gold and peach rays of setting sun and the sounds of Julia's high-pitched giggles and the low rumble of Nic's laughter drifted through the open windows. The mere thought of him filled Elizabeth with radiance. Longing filled her, too. She longed for the closeness they shared when they were married and made love.

Elizabeth looked up from loading the dishwasher. Vie's face was lined with worry. "You look pale. Do you need to sit down?'

"No, I am fine," Vie answered.

"You don't look all right." Elizabeth abandoned the dishwasher to come closer. Vie gripped the edge of the counter, feeling the wave of nausea wash over her. Elizabeth insisted, "Go sit down in the living room and put your feet up. I'll finish up in here."

"I felt a little nauseous, dear, but I am fine. Besides, I am not going to leave you with the cleanup. It is the least I can do for you feeding me." Vie snatched the towel from the counter and continued to wipe it down.

That Vie. She had a stubborn streak. Bless her.

After everyone left, it had taken quite a bit of effort to get Julia settled down, bathed and in her bed for the night. She had finally drifted off to sleep as Elizabeth read from her favorite storybook.

Elizabeth sat down at the dining table with a cup of green tea and her devotional. She studied the page, focusing on one of her favorite verses. *I wait for the Lord, my soul waits, and in His word I put my hope.* She might be longing for Nic, but she had to have patience and give God time to work in their lives.

Chapter Eleven

Elizabeth faced another day, remembering those quiet mornings before Julia was born when she had time for devotional reading and reflection over her morning cup of coffee. Now her mornings were filled with constant noise and motion. She blew strands of hair out of her eyes and opened the closet door.

"Look mommy, I'm a bird." Julia stuck out her arms as if she was flying.

Elizabeth snagged her around the waist and snuggled her close. The little girl squealed with anticipation. Elizabeth gave the lightest of tickles to her daughter's tummy as she wiggled and laughed.

"All right, what is going on in here?" Nic filled the doorway.

"Mommy is tickling me."

"Is that right? Well, I am afraid I can't let this go on." He came into the room, moving quickly. "Not without me!"

"No, Daddy!" Julia's protests dissolved into more happy squeals as Nic tickled her.

Elizabeth felt her heart fall again for this man. Love wasn't a sum of every past moment of shared history. She had not realized that before, because she had always thought that it was their devotion to one another, day by day, that built upon itself to make their marriage a strong one.

"Daddy, I want a puppy or a kitty cat!" Julia burst out.

Elizabeth ruffled her fingers through her daughter's hair and gave Nic a warning look as if to say, "Don't even think about it."

His eyes glimmered back at her. "I don't know; it might be good for her to have a pet."

"Nic!" Elizabeth sighed. But one look at Julia's pleading eyes, all the reasons why now was not the right time faded.

"All right." She said those dreaded words, hardly getting the last one out before Julia shouted in triumph and Nic gave her a loud smacking kiss on the cheek. Lord help her, she had never been able to say no to this man. The man she now loved more, impossibly more, for how hard he had fought to come back to her. Their past no longer mattered. Love was so much more than where they had been or where they were going. It was where they were now.

Elizabeth had never imagined the heartbreak in the eyes of the rows and rows of kennels at the local animal shelter. There were numerous cats, big dogs, little dogs, and in-between sized dogs all with big, soulful eyes. From the moment they stepped foot into the narrow aisle, nearly all the animals raced to the front of their cages, offering friendly meows, excited yips, or loud barks as if they were saying, "Look at me!"

Nic's hand settled on her shoulder. "How are we ever going to choose one?"

"I don't know," Elizabeth replied. "Because that means we are saying no to all of the other ones." She knew little about cats and dogs, never having owned one of her own. There certainly seemed to be some nice ones, like the big yellow Labrador retriever pressed against the metal cage trying to get his tongue on Julia's hand.

"Stay here with Mommy." Elizabeth held on to her daughter's hand firmly now. "We don't want to startle any of the animals."

Julia pulled hard to get free. "Look at the curly one!"

An older looking, white poodle seated in the next kennel panted, as if trying to make friends.

"Oh, look at the brown one!"

In the kennel next door, a chocolate Labrador jumped excitedly, trying to steal the attention.

A few steps ahead, Nic stood in the aisle, contemplating all of the options.

"Mommy, that's the one!" Julia yelled out, pointing to a black and white cat. Her loudness seemed like an invitation for all the animals to make more noise. And as the barks echoed and a caretaker ordered them to hush, Julia gave a mighty yank from Elizabeth's grasp and went down on her knees in front of the cage. The cat pressed his face against her small hand and licked happily. Julia was pink with delight.

"Mommy, this is him! This is the one I want!"

A long list of why this might not be the best choice rolled into Elizabeth's mind and onto the tip of her tongue, but Nic's firm grip on her shoulder tightened just a little.

"I think this is a good choice," he said in that resolute way of his, stepping over to Julia and the cat who was doing his best to win everyone's affections.

Nic had been raised around pets, so Elizabeth trusted his decision. He knelt down and began rubbing what he could of the cat's head through the metal barrier. "You are a good boy, aren't you?"

The cat meowed loudly and licked Nic's hand as if he was answering his question.

"I love him!" Julia announced with contentment, her mind — no her heart — made up. "Mommy, he licked my hand!" She wiped her hand across the front of her Disney t-shirt to dry it off, but she was still pink with joy.

Nic, Julia and the cat glared at Elizabeth, all powerfully pleading. No words were necessary. Not a single one. From Julia's pleading to Nic's silent nod, and the cat's big green eyes that were filled with so much sadness, she felt her resistance buckle. She had enough on her plate without falling in love with a cat but that seemed to have happened.

An hour and a half later, Nic was driving toward home with all four of them in the Range Rover — Elizabeth, Julia, himself and a cat. The newest member of the family had curled up at Julia's feet, purring; the sounds were rising and falling, as if he were content. "He sure is glad to have found his forever home," Elizabeth commented as she reached back and petted the cat's head.

Nic, behind the wheel, flashed a grin and spoke in a hushed tone. "At least she has forgotten to protest about the car seat. See, having a pet is a good thing."

"Yes, I guess so," Elizabeth replied, trying not to laugh.

"There's Dairy Queen. How about we pick up lunch?" Nic asked.

"Sure." Elizabeth was quick to agree.

When they went around to the drive-through, Julia insisted on an extra hot dog for Kitty Kat, as she was now referring to the cat. And the cat meowed continuously from the moment he smelled the bagged food.

"Homeward bound," Nic said, as he pulled out onto the roadway. "Unless there is anywhere else the lady wants to go?"

"Oh, I can think of a few places," she replied. "Just the two of us."

"You would miss Julia before the plane got off the ground." Nic smiled at her, so handsome even with his lopsided grin.

"That is true."

He stopped for a red light and for a long moment, his gaze held hers with unashamed intensity. It was good to be with him again. And when she glanced over her shoulder at Julia and Kitty Kat, they both looked happy.

"You are lucky, you know that," Elizabeth said to the cat and she couldn't help patting his head again. His short hair was warm and velvety, and he pressed ardently against her touch. It was impossible not to adore him.

The afternoon was crazy, of course. She should have anticipated that, Elizabeth chided herself as she answered her cell phone. "Hello?"

"It's Spencer. Got a minute?" Typical Spencer, barking out what sounded like an order when it should have been a polite question.

"Yes, I have a minute," she replied as she ran out of her bedroom and down the hallway, following the trail of Julia and the cat.

"Do you want a full time job?"

"A full time job? Are you kidding me?"

"No, I am dead serious. But since you don't sound thrilled, how about this? You set your own hours into the schedule. How is that?"

"It was good timing, considering the stack of bills growing on the counter." She caught a glimpse of Julia pushing open the back door. "Let me talk it over with Nic."

"Sure. I just thought you could use the income. I know Nic has disability insurance but it can't compare to what he was making. Besides, I could use your help."

Up ahead, Julia and the cat slipped through the door. "Spencer, how about we talk about this on Sunday? You can come over for lunch after church."

"Okay. Talk to you then." The line clicked off.

Elizabeth squinted against the bright glare of sunshine and swooped down to sweep Julia off her feet in mid-stride.

"Mommy!" The little girl squealed.

Elizabeth kissed Julia's cheek, hoping to offset a temper tantrum. "You are supposed to be taking a nap, princess."

"But I want to play with Kitty Kat!" her voice thin and high as she rubbed her tired eyes.

"Kitty Kat has to take a nap, too."

Elizabeth closed the door and headed down the hallway. It was not easy keeping hold of a wiggling toddler, but she had gotten the knack of it. "No, mommy!" echoed in the hallway around her.

"Shhh, baby," Elizabeth cooed, gently as she turned into Julia's room, curtains drawn against the bright sun. She eased onto the corner of the bed. "I will read more from your favorite story."

"I want to go outside with Kitty Kat. Please?" The little girl gave a tiny sob of misery.

Elizabeth could not resist holding her baby girl and rocking her. Julia's arms wrapped around her neck and held on.

The alarm system chimed, announcing the front door had opened. Was it Vie already? Or had Nic come early? Her whole being seemed to still, listening for the sound of footsteps.

Vie, she realized, when she heard the click of heels on the tile. "Back here," Elizabeth called out.

The elderly lady appeared in the doorway, looking lovely and fresh as a summer's day with her gray hair pulled back in a bun. "Someone's up from their nap."

"She never went down for one." Elizabeth kissed her daughter's head, trying to soothe her, rocking her back and forth. "We have had way too much excitement today."

Vie nodded, stepping into the room, her arms out. "Let me read her a story. How about I read a story to you, princess?"

"How are you doing?" Elizabeth asked as she handed her daughter over.

Vie took Julia lovingly and snuggled her close. "I am doing fine. Don't worry about me, not when you and Nic have an evening planned."

Elizabeth's hopes were high. How could they not be? She was going out with the only man who had ever owned her heart. "Oh—there he is!"

"Go, I've got Julia." Vie nodded over the top of the little girl's curls. "You aren't even dressed yet!"

Elizabeth looked down at the T-shirt and denims she had on. She definitely had to shower and change clothes.

Nic now stood in the foyer, dressed in dark trousers and a crisp, white shirt. Caught in the act of setting a crystal vase of a dozen long-stemmed red roses on the entry table, he shot her a sheepish grin. She felt her breath catch. She moved toward him without thought, as if her spirit led her to his side. "Hello, handsome."

"Hello, babe," his baritone voice dipped low, intimate. "I have missed you."

She went up on tiptoe to kiss him. A sense of rightness poured through her soul. "I have missed you so much. Give me some time to get ready and I'm all yours."

Chapter Twelve

Their dinner at the highly acclaimed L'etoile had gone perfectly, Nic was thankful for that. And now, watching the look on Elizabeth's face, as they rose up into the sky on the carnival Ferris wheel, he knew he had done well by her standards.

He had wanted this evening to be special, as he had learned that they had gone to the carnival on their first date. The pressure was on because he wanted this time to be even better than the first time around.

Elizabeth's slender hand held to the side of the seat they were in. "It looks like you did your homework, mister."

He inched a little closer to her. "Vie reminded me about the dozen long stem roses and the carnival. And Justen suggested that I take you to L'etoile for dinner." He admitted these things unashamed that he could not remember the first date they shared.

"This is magical." Elizabeth tipped her head, the ocean breeze catching her hair and lifting it away from her face so that Nic saw her clearly; every contour, every hope. Suspended in the cool air, she had never felt more terrified or more certain of anything in her life.

"Justen also told me that I am supposed to do something monumental."

Humor warmed her eyes. "You mean like bungee jumping?"

"Yes." Nic quipped. "But I think that this time I should choose a more romantic approach, and so I will save that for the big finale."

"Oh, so you have a big finale planned, do you? That sounds promising."

"Those were my thoughts exactly." He suddenly felt as shy as he had been during their first date. They had spent dinner talking over the events of the past few weeks...Julia, Kitty Kat, their friends and family. He felt closer to her than he had in a long time. But he did not know how to tell Elizabeth what mattered. How his heart was alive with devotion for her. He couldn't tell her that being with her made the sky bluer, the sun brighter, and his spirit as light as the wind against them.

He didn't need the past. He didn't need a single memory because he was with her now. He adored the way she gazed up at him with unabashed affection. And the way she leaned a little closer to him. The dreams in her eyes were as real as the silent question in his mind.

Somehow he had to find a way to tell her how he felt. "The doctors were right. I am not going to remember the past." There he had said it. He waited, heart hammering against his chest, while sadness filled her eyes. They had been functioning under the hope and belief that he would one day remember the life they had shared, that he would remember because she needed him to.

Now the truth was out in the open. It was not going to happen. Would she still want him? Or was it over for the two of them? His soul ached at the thought. Falling out of the Ferris wheel ride and hitting the ground far below would be less painful than losing her again.

"I know." Elizabeth sounded sad, but not shocked. She did not turn away from him. "But we can go on from her. We can make new memories."

Relief rushed through him like a jet stream. "I will do all I can to make them the best memories ever," he vowed.

"I know that you will, Nic."

It helped to see her faith in him there on her beautiful face. They would go on from here and that was something that he could do. He took her hands in his. "I might not remember, but I know how I must have felt all those years ago standing before you just like this. My heart is racing and my pulse is pounding. I can hardly think and talk at the same time."

She smiled, her eyes going soft with affection, and more hope than he could measure. He wanted to be the man she needed. To be everything she needed. He paused, searching for the words. "Something tells me that back then I loved you first. That the moment I saw you walking near the pier, I knew that I was going to marry you."

"Yes, it was love at first sight," she reassured him, once they had stepped off the ride and began walking hand in hand.

"I know that I want to be the one man you can always count on, who would never let you down."

"Nic, I hope that you don't think you have done that." Her gaze searched his with pure honesty.

She might not realize how he had failed her. How Spencer had offered her a full-time job because he could no longer support the family. Yes, he believed that she truly did not see his failures. But he did. And that she loved him still meant more to him that she would ever know.

"Nic, I know that this has been hard for you. Julia and I were strangers to you, and I..." She stopped, searching for the right words to say. His hand holding hers did not let go. "I know that it will take a lot of time for you to love me again."

"No, you are wrong." His hand released hers to touch the side of her face, cradling her gently. His gaze deepened and focused on her lips. He leaned in closer and she felt as if her pulse stopped and her soul stilled in anticipation as she waited for the first brush of his lips to hers. And for the first tenderness of his kiss.

Everything within her seemed to melt when his lips covered hers in a warm velvet brush. Suspended between their past and their future, time stood still. She was lost in his kiss, in being closer to this new Nic than she had ever been before.

The wind swirled around them and Nic pulled away, but he did not let her go. He held her close, the distance between them as good as gone. For that moment, it felt as if they had never been apart. As if nothing between them had ever changed. Her hope was now that this closeness would never end.

"So," he murmured against her ear. "Did I sweep you off your feet?"

"You most definitely did that!" she exclaimed, letting herself lean against him and savor being safe in his arms once again.

They were pulling into the driveway and Elizabeth suspected that she still hadn't managed to touch the ground yet. Her hopes were sky-high and her heart floating because it was so full. All her troubles felt far away and so small, they hardly mattered. What did matter — what would always matter — was the way Nic was gazing at her with deep affection in his eyes. He loved her. He had not said the words yet, but they were in the air between them. Then he leaned closer to hold the back of her head and slant his lips to hers. His kiss was passionate and tender, just as it always had been. Elizabeth was so wrapped up in his love, that all of the hardship of the past year would be washed away. There was only the two of them and their love.

"I don't want this night to end," she whispered against his lips, barely breaking their kiss.

There was so much emotion in his eyes, deep and intimate. She brushed her fingertips along the edge of his angular jaw. It was wonderful feeling as if they were in sync again.

"We don't have to let it end," he told her with a smile.

She nodded once, in agreement perhaps, and gave him one more kiss. "It is getting late. We had better go in. Vie must be wondering what we are doing sitting in the Range Rover."

He got out of the seat and circled around to open her door. When he looked at her he felt whole, as if he had never been broken by his injury.

Vie was waiting for them, the kitchen clean and tidy, Julia's toys picked up and put away. "Kitty Kat is on the foot of Julia's bed. I could not get him to budge," she said with a smile.

Elizabeth could not help laughing. "It is okay." She felt so good with Nic at her side, his hand on her lower back. Not only was he physically close, but he was emotionally close, too.

Vie turned to pick up her cardigan and purse and made her way to the door. "I'll go and leave you two alone," her voice low to keep from waking Julia.

"Uh, we will talk later, then." Elizabeth called out. But it was too late, the door was closed and Vie was gone leaving her alone with Nic.

"I will check on Julia before I leave," his rich baritone was nothing but tender. She watched him as he took one step from her, then another, and another until the shadows of the hallway claimed him.

Nic made his way back from Julia's bedroom. Across the room, his gaze found Elizabeth's and there was that dear smile that tugged at her heart. She could still feel the pull of his heart to hers and the connection of the emotions they shared. Standing before him, vulnerable, with her heart wide-open, she waited for the words that she needed to hear.

"I love you, Elizabeth." He said quietly as he pulled her into his strong arms.

"I love you, more," she whispered before Nic's lips found hers.

Chapter Thirteen

Nic rubbed his face dry with the towel, feeling great about how the night before turned out. He had done everything he could to make Elizabeth happy. He hated that it was not enough, as it once had been.

He hated that she had to take the full-time job Spencer had offered her. But before long, he intended to be back at work. Not in the hockey rink; he would probably never play again, but he would be glad to go back as a coach or team manager. Soon, he promised himself, he would work to make that happen.

He had so much to be thankful for. God had allowed Elizabeth to come back to him. She was the reason he found strength to breathe every morning. Her love was what had driven him before in that life that he could not remember and it drove him now.

"Elizabeth!" He looked up, startled, when she appeared in the doorway. Lost in his thoughts, he hadn't heard her come in. "Hi!" She smiled her usual big smile as she said it.

Bare feet padded across the tile and suddenly Julia's little arms wrapped around Nic's leg. "Daddy, I want kisses!"

The cat had been right on her heels and now stood there meowing. "She insisted that we bring him."

Nic pulled Julia in his arms and cradled her, so small and fragile feeling, wishing he could keep her right here until he could prove to her that he was the father she deserved. Over the top of Julia's curls, Nic winked at Elizabeth. Moments later, Julia was giggling and running out of the room with Kitty Kat close behind her.

Elizabeth reached up and placed her hands against the sides of Nic's face. Her touch sent hope coursing to his soul. "No one told you what yesterday was, right?"

Her question stumped him. He shook his head.

"I did everything Vie and Justen said I should do."

"They probably thought that you already knew. Yesterday was — would have been — our anniversary."

"Oh, I am sorry. I did not know." How could he have forgotten that? He felt his insides turn cold.

"We would have been married for five years. I was so happy to be your wife, Nic."

Panic struck him like a speeding truck. She was talking in past tense. His injury had cost him so much, precious memories that he could never get back. He was not about to let it take Elizabeth from him, again. He had fought so hard for her, but it had been in all the wrong ways. His need to be whole and strong for her that was for himself, he could see that now. "I did not remember. I should have. I'm sorry."

"I know, Nic. I just expected that you would remember seeing the date in the photo album. Maybe I have been wrong all along." She looked so lost, as lost as he felt.

"Please, give me the chance to make it up to you."

"We had a nice evening. That was enough. It was..."

"Elizabeth, don't give up on me...on us." I am begging you." Anger filled him; anger towards the man who had forced him into the glass and struck him in the head with the hockey stick. Pointless anger he had to let go of.

"I'm not going to give up, Nic. I need you. I love you. From the moment I got that call, I was terrified I would lose you. Until I saw you unconscious on that hospital bed, I didn't realize that you were my strength, my heart, my everything."

He brushed the hair out of her eyes so that he could look into them. "You are everything to me. I love you." Nic said softly. His gaze fastened on hers as if he were seeing deep into her heart and into the secret places of her soul. "I am in love with you. I think about losing you and my world crashes into pieces. I am nothing without you."

"Nic, that is exactly how I feel." She let him draw her into his arms, where she belonged. She savored the feeling of being close to him. His lips found hers with infinite passion. His kiss was more than a promise it was perfection.

When he broke off the kiss, he took her hand in his. "I want a wedding I can remember. Let me promise to love and honor you again. Will you marry me?'

"Oh, Nic, I would be honored to be your wife." She kissed him once again.

"I promise I will love you for the rest of my life. I will do everything I can to be the husband you need."

"I know that, Nic." She felt pure joy sift into her heart, like sand on a sun-kissed shore at the ocean's end.

Chapter Fourteen

Two weeks later, Elizabeth stood and peered through the bedroom window of her house into the sun-swept backyard full of her family and friends. Blooming roses adorned the garden and the arbor, where Nic was waiting for her. He looked so handsome in his black tuxedo. Her heart overflowed with happiness from simply gazing upon him.

Her mother, Grace, waltzed in the room, lovely as always. "Oh, you look beautiful. Where are the girls?"

"They are around here somewhere," Elizabeth answered, stepping away from the window but keeping him in sight. Nic was chatting with their pastor, who had squeezed them into the schedule, despite the busy wedding season here on the island. It had not been easy planning a wedding so quickly but it had been a labor of love.

"This might not be your first wedding, but it is a real one nonetheless. We can't go bucking tradition." Vie stepped over to brush at her hair and straighten the veil. "You look nervous dear. Take a deep breath. It is going to be just fine."

"I know. It is silly feeling like this." She glanced at the beveled mirror above her bureau. The woman staring back at her was swathed in the white silk of a wedding dress, but she was no longer that young starry-eyed bride from their first wedding photos.

Time and the challenges of life had changed her. There were a few lines on her face and she had a more mature look. The love she felt for Nic had changed, too. Tested by fire, purified in the process, it was stronger than ever before. While their bond had been sound before, it was invincible now. Nic's injury had been a blessing in disguise.

Heels tapped down the hallway and Sue, in her turquoise bridesmaid dress, appeared in the doorway. "I have the penny for your shoe so off with it Elizabeth."

"Like that is easy to do in this dress." She couldn't help laughing as she searched through the silk and ruffles for her white satin shoes and was grateful when Vie bent to remove the shoe. Elizabeth stood on one foot, holding on the back of a nearby chair, while Sue placed the penny in her shoe. Then she wiggled her foot back into the slipper.

"I have got something that is both old and borrowed." Michel, newly married to Justen, swept into the room in her bridesmaid dress holding something small in her hand. "I have mother's gold cross."

Emotion burned in Elizabeth's eyes as she bent down, holding up her hair so that Michel could latch the delicate gold necklace. When she straightened up, the beautiful jeweled cross gleamed like the sun. It had been a wedding gift to Vie from Walter, and it was like a sign that this new phase of marriage would be as blessed as their fifty years together had been.

Her mother rustled back into the room and handed over a small box. "I have something blue." Elizabeth took the box out of her mother's hand and opened it slowly. She fingered the quality, beautifully designed sapphire ring.

"It is so beautiful. But Mother you did not have to get this for me."

"Oh, my dear, I know I didn't have to, but I wanted to. I know how you have adored jewelry since you were Julia's age."

As if on cue, Julia, who was the flower girl, burst into the room. "You look so pretty, Mommy!"

"And so do you my princess." Elizabeth straightened her daughter's tiara — the one she insisted on wearing - and gave her a smacking kiss on the cheek.

"It is time to go dear." Elizabeth's mother took her hand to steady her. She let her mother help her with the dress and train as she made her way to the back doorway. While she waited for her bridesmaids to precede her down the aisle between the rows of folding chairs, she was joined by Justen, who was going to give her away.

"Now I need you to walk straight down that aisle to your daddy, okay?" She said to Julia.

"Okay, Mommy!"

But of course, Julia stopped on her way down the aisle, twirling until her dress spun out around her and she came to a dizzy stop.

Then it was her turn. Everyone stood to watch as Elizabeth stepped out into the sunlight on Justen's arm. The presence of the onlookers, the lull of the music from a hired string quartet, the beauty of the backyard and her own nerves faded to nothing. All she saw was the handsome man waiting for her at the arbor. His gaze was only for her, his eyes never left hers as she took each step, closing the distance between them.

The ocean breeze stirred the warm air and the fragrance from the many roses. Michel stepped forward to take her bouquet. She took the flowers and gave her friend a kiss on the cheek. Julia was spinning more circles and Sue was quietly trying to get her to stop.

Nic reached out to take her hand. The moment she laid her fingers on his wide palm her entire being sighed with relief. "You are my beloved," he whispered in her ear, holding on to her as if he never intended to let her go. "All ways and always."

"And you are mine, Nic."

When Elizabeth looked at Nic's best man, Jaryl Gronkowski, she knew that God had taken a terrible tragedy; an act committed by the same man standing next to Nic, and worked it out for His good.

Independence Day
Excerpt

Martha's Vineyard has become one of the Northeast's most prominent summering havens, having attracted numerous U.S. presidents and A-list celebrities. Its gorgeous beaches and secluded hideaways have been cherished by generations, including the Chamberlain family. Phoenix Chamberlain, III, comes from a wealthy family and has vacationed in Martha's Vineyard every summer since he was a young boy. The fact that his wife, Sierra Ramstad Chamberlain was from a middle-class family, their backgrounds were different. Growing up, her idea of vacation was a fishing trip to the lake with a sack lunch.

Sierra stepped onto the back porch and surveyed the lush green lawn. The myriad of flowers lining the white picket fence looked pristine and provided a striking contrast to the golden sand and sparkling sea beyond. She had an eye for beauty and appreciated the blending of heights and colors and texture that spoke of careful planning. She made her way down the steps, and gazed at the plants and flowers as their blooms reached for the sky.

As if on cue, Phoenix and Preston appeared from around the far side of the cottage. Taken back, Sierra stopped in her tracks. "It's lovely here, she announced as she glanced around.

"Yes, it is," Phoenix agreed as he wrapped his arm around her shoulders.

Phoenix cast a wary eye at the clouds massing on the horizon as he, Sierra and Preston walked down Main Street. The clouds had begun to gather while they played on the beach earlier and they'd grown more ominous during their brief stop at their cottage. If they continued to build, he suspected the fireworks would be curtailed this evening.

Phoenix ascended the steps to the porch of the restaurant, high on a bluff on the outskirts of town, and paused with Rylee Claire in his arm, to take in the sweeping view of the ocean. He pushed the door open and they stepped inside the restaurant, already packed for dinner. In his beige slacks, navy blue sport coat and open-necked white shirt, Phoenix looked preppy and very handsome.

Phoenix, Sierra, and Preston followed the hostess to the white linen covered table by the window that offered a panoramic view of the ocean. After Sierra took her seat, Phoenix handed her Rylee Claire who stifled a gasp. Once Preston was seated, Phoenix took his seat and opened the menu the waiter handed him. "We will have your best wine," he said to the waiter before he turned to walk away.

Although it was informal, Sierra's attire reeked of class – and money. Her blond hair was swept back in a chic chignon. Phoenix winked at her and her heart skipped a beat.

"I will order an appetizer while we wait," he said, now that he had her attention.

"Sure, thank you," Sierra replied.

A woman pushed through the door and dashed across the crowded room. Sierra had to look twice to recognize the woman waving to her. But it was Sue Deveroux, all right, her face creased in a smile, and her raven black hair pulled up in a ponytail that swung like a pendulum behind her. She was wearing a beige skirt, a white cotton blouse and brown leather sandals. Her ruggedly handsome husband, Spencer, followed close behind her.

Excitement had put a becoming flush on Sue's cheeks, and her onyx eyes were shining. But it was clear from Phoenix's narrowed-eyed expression that he didn't share her excitement. Sue was going to counseling in an attempt to deal with the lifetime of abuse she had received from her father and she was making progress. It helped that she had an amazing husband to show her how she should be loved and respected.

Sue and Spencer had kept in touch with Phoenix and Sierra but this would be the first time that Sue saw Preston since her departure from Seaside Haven. As Preston's adoptive parents, it was only natural for Phoenix and Sierra to be a little wary of the situation.

Spencer shook hands with Phoenix and nodded to Sierra who found herself pulled into a hug with Sue. "May I hold Preston?" Sue asked, when she let go of Sierra.

The waiter returned with the bottle of wine, saving Sierra from having to reply. And Phoenix avoided the question entirely by placing the order for an appetizer.

Seconds later, Justen and Michel Sonni Ben-David made their entrance. Sierra gave them a quick sweep. Michel had sleek blond hair and a girl-next-door smile. The chic, designer clothes she wore couldn't hide the extra twenty pounds on her small frame. But that was understandable; after all she was expecting her first child. She did look a bit younger than Sierra had expected. Botox, no doubt, she noted.

Sue gave Michel air kisses in the direction of each cheek and waited for Michel to follow her lead while the men shook hands. Sierra thought that if either woman's smile had been drawn any tighter their glossy lips would have disappeared altogether.

Sierra didn't stand to greet them but she did extend her hand. "It's so nice to meet you."

Michel took Sierra's hand, briefly, and said, "Likewise."

Sierra gestured to the sleeping child in her lap. "Peace reigns once again."

The room had gone silent, Sierra realized, as she looked down at Rylee Claire. As she focused on the sleeping child, tears formed in her eyes. Each finger was so tiny, yet so perfect.

The door opened once more and Nic, Elizabeth and Julia Ben-David joined the group gathered in the rear of the restaurant. As they drew close, Sierra saw the resemblance of Justen and Nic at once. They both had a lean build and broad shoulders. Elizabeth was a slender woman with long, reddish-brown hair. Her silk dress was the hue of blue hydrangeas. Nic wore a wheat-colored sport coat with dark slacks and a light blue shirt. Young Preston Chamberlain was delighted to see someone close to his age, as Julia smiled and waved.

Phoenix was introducing Sierra to Nic and Elizabeth when the waiter delivered the appetizer and handed everyone a menu. "I will give you some time to look over the menu."

Laughter and soft music drifted across the room and everyone at the table resumed chatting when the waiter departed. Phoenix and Sierra was both relieved and surprised at the transformation that seemed to have taken place in Sue.

After a few minutes, the waiter returned and diverted the conversation. "Are you ready to order?" As they placed their orders, they handed over their menus.

Light conversation took them through their salads and up to the delivery of their entrees. Everyone seemed to be indulging in their meal; except Michel who poked at her seared halibut as a wave of nausea swept over her. Justen reached out and covered one of her hands with his. Startled, she lifted her chin to meet his gaze. In his eyes she saw compassion – but also concern. As if he sensed something was amiss. Although the temptation to simply get up and walk out was strong, she refrained.

Various innocuous topics carried them through the entrée portion of the meal. As dinner wound down, the waiter hovered over their shoulders and whisked their plates away. Another waiter appeared carrying a cake with flickering candles on top. He sat it in front of Phoenix.

"What's a birthday without a cake? Make a wish," Sierra said.

Michel folded her hands in her lap as she glared at the cake.

"Shall we sing?" Elizabeth asked.

And the whole crew sang an off-key rendition of 'Happy Birthday' to Phoenix.

As Justen ate his last bite of cake, he took a quick look at Michel. She'd eaten no more than a forkful of her dessert. And she'd grown increasingly more subdued as the meal had progressed. He supposed it was the pregnancy that was responsible for the pall that had fallen over her.

Beside him, Sierra set her napkin on the table and Phoenix reached for Rylee Claire. "It's been lovely meeting you all." She directed her comment to those seated around the table. She rose, and Phoenix immediately did the same. Nic and Elizabeth weren't far behind.

"We better get going or we'll miss the fireworks," Nic reminded them.

At Nic's comment, Michel turned to look at Justen. A look of dread flashed across her face. "I'm not sure if I feel up to going."

He set his napkin on the table and stood up. "I'll drive you home."

With another stiff smile, Michel eased past him and headed for the door. Justen was close on her heels. There was a flurry of conversation in the restaurant, followed by the cough of Justen's truck engine as it turned over.

Once outside in the deepening twilight, Phoenix surveyed the dark clouds overhead. "It looks like we're in for a storm."

"Yes, I hope we make it home before it hits."

Sierra fell into step beside Phoenix, who was holding an awakened Rylee Claire, as they walked down the path toward the bluff above the beach. Nic, Elizabeth, Sue and Spencer followed behind them as Julia and Preston giggled and ran along beside them.

Surprisingly the rain did not come, although the sky remained overcast. From the moment they arrived to see the fireworks, Spencer had hold of Sue's hand. And from the first time he meet her, he'd known he wanted to spend the rest of his life with her.

Phoenix held Rylee Claire in one arm casually resting the other across Sierra's shoulders. Preston leaned against her leg and Julia stood next to him. The skies lit up with a kaleidoscope of green and gold and red and blue, and the glowing remains floated down into the bay.

Nic and Elizabeth had been through a lot since Nic's accident in the hockey rink, but their love for one another had stood the test of time and they had never been happier. They kissed, vaguely aware of the sky turning red, blue and golden as the grand finale of fireworks exploded.

"I thought we'd take a walk on the beach," Phoenix suggested. "The others said they would watch the kids for a little while."

He led the way to a deck and stairway to the beach. When he reached for Sierra's hand to guide her around a cluster of sea oats that had grown up through the slits of the boardwalk, she didn't resist. Then when they reached the relatively level surface of the beach it was perfectly natural to just keep holding her hand. Silence descended upon them, except for the rhythmic pounding of the surf.

The night was balmy and a full moon peeked through the clouds giving an ethereal glow to the beach, as Sierra gazed out over the shimmering sea. With Phoenix's hand in hers, the gentle breeze on her cheeks, and the moon silvering the world around her, she said a silent prayer of thanks heavenward.

Also Available by Sandra W. Burch

POETIC INJUSTICE

COLLECTIVE SOUL

SEASIDE HAVEN

AWAY FROM THE SUN

REMEMBER ME